MONTANA MAVERICKS

Welcome to Big Sky Country, home of the Montana Mavericks! Where free-spirited men and women discover love on the range...

BROTHERS AND BRONCOS

Romance is in the air for the ranchers of Bronco, but someone is watching from the sidelines. A man from the town's past could be behind the mysterious messages, but does he pose a threat to Bronco's future? With their happily-ever-afters at stake, the bighearted cowboys will do what it takes to protect their beloved town— and the women they can't live without!

THANKFUL FOR THE MAVERICK

Rancher Garrett Abernathy thinks he enjoys his quiet Montana life—until rodeo rider Brynn Hawkins comes to town and changes everything. Brynn is full of laughter and makes Garrett long for things he gave up on after his divorce ten years ago. But her rising career inevitably means she'll be off on the road again soon, and Garrett fears repeating old mistakes and losing himself to love...

Dear Reader,

When I was invited to contribute to the Montana Mavericks, I realized I had to step up my game to immerse myself into this incredibly popular continuity. I began reading the books in the previous cycle and attended a live rodeo. It was only after I had transitioned from watching documentaries to the Cowboy and Country Music Television channels and *Living Big Sky* on Destination America that I felt confident enough to write *Thankful for the Maverick*.

Rancher Garrett Abernathy is happy that his brothers are engaged, but for him, marriage is been there, done that. After his ten-year marriage ended in divorce, he promised himself never to leave Bronco—or fall in love again. But everything changes when he's introduced to Brynn Hawkins of the famous Hawkins Sisters. Although he finds himself enthralled with the beautiful, talented rodeo star, he knows they could never have a future together. Her life with the rodeo keeps her on the move—while his feet are firmly planted—and he believes she's too young for a man in his forties.

Brynn isn't looking for a relationship, but when she meets Garrett, she can sense there's something different about him. Their connection is instantaneous, and Brynn knows she wants Garrett to be the only man in her life. However, there's something keeping them from taking the next step: his reluctance to talk about his failed marriage. What will it take for the spitfire rodeo rider to melt the maverick's heart—and for them to find their happily-ever-after?

I hope you will enjoy *Thankful for the Maverick* as much as I enjoyed writing about the unforgettable characters that make Bronco, Montana, so memorable.

Happy reading!

Rochelle Alers

Special thanks and acknowledgment are given to
Rochelle Alers for her contribution to the
Montana Mavericks: Brothers & Broncos miniseries.

Recycling programs
for this product may
not exist in your area.

ISBN-13: 978-1-335-72426-7

Thankful for the Maverick

Copyright © 2022 by Harlequin Enterprises ULC

For questions and comments about the quality of this book,
please contact us at CustomerService@Harlequin.com.

Harlequin Enterprises ULC
22 Adelaide St. West, 41st Floor
Toronto, Ontario M5H 4E3, Canada
www.Harlequin.com

Printed in U.S.A.

Thankful for the Maverick

ROCHELLE ALERS

HARLEQUIN
SPECIAL
EDITION

Since 1988, nationally bestselling author **Rochelle Alers** has written more than eighty books and short stories. She has earned numerous honors, including the Zora Neale Hurston Award, the Vivian Stephens Award for Excellence in Romance Writing and a Career Achievement Award from *RT Book Reviews*. She is a member of Zeta Phi Beta Sorority, Inc., Iota Theta Zeta Chapter. A full-time writer, she lives in a charming hamlet on Long Island. Rochelle can be contacted through her website, www.rochellealers.org.

Books by Rochelle Alers

Harlequin Special Edition

Bainbridge House

A New Foundation
Christmas at the Chateau

Furever Yours

The Bookshop Rescue

Wickham Falls Weddings

Home to Wickham Falls
Her Wickham Falls SEAL
The Sheriff of Wickham Falls
Dealmaker, Heartbreaker
This Time for Keeps
Second-Chance Sweet Shop

American Heroes

Claiming the Captain's Baby
Twins for the Soldier

Visit the Author Profile page
at Harlequin.com for more titles.

This book is dedicated to the talented and skilled Black cowboys and cowgirls who compete in the Bill Pickett Invitational Rodeo.

Chapter One

Garrett Abernathy didn't need to set an alarm to wake up; his internal clock told him it was time to get out of bed and head out to check on the fence lines, cattle, horses and bison on the Flying A Ranch before driving to the Bronco Convention Center to meet with the manager. He'd set up an appointment with Chuck Carter to discuss adding organic bison burgers to the catering menu for the Mistletoe Rodeo scheduled for later in the week.

Last year the excitement in Bronco was akin to that of Super Bowl Sunday when Bronco's own champion bronc rider, Geoff Burris, was the emcee and was also on the program. The rodeo had brought in crowds from all over Montana and neighboring states to watch professional as well as amateurs exhibit their skills in the three-day event. Now there was even more excitement because the organizers had announced the Hawkins Sisters were also on the card.

Earlier in the year, Garrett had attended the Bronco Summer Family Rodeo, and he had only caught a glimpse of the women during their performances. He might be an armchair spectator when it came to baseball, basketball or hockey, but for the rodeo, he had to be at the action.

However, making certain his family's cattle ranch remained viable had become a top priority for Garrett. At the age of forty-three, the eldest of Hutch and Hannah's five sons had returned to Bronco ten years ago, after his divorce, and thrown all his energies into what he loved most—the family business.

The small herd of bison were a new addition to the livestock. Though their father had been skeptical at first, Garrett and his four brothers were confident that the distribution of organic bison meat to restaurants was a win-win proposition. When they had purchased the bison, eleven heifers were already pregnant and this past spring new calves had increased the herd to forty-three.

It was midmorning by the time he'd completed his inspections and Garrett returned home to prepare for his meeting with Chuck.

The border collie puppy he'd adopted earlier that year from the Happy Hearts Animal Sanctuary began whining as a cleaned-up Garrett slipped his arms into the sleeves of a corduroy jacket. It was on a rare occasion that Garrett did not wear the jacket. It had be-

come so much of a favorite garment for him that he'd purchased several in navy blue and chocolate brown. Once one wore out, he'd exchange it for a newer one. It was a favored alternative to the suits he'd worn when living and working in New York, suits that had begun to feel like straitjackets.

He shook his head at the whining pup. "Not now, Max. When I come back, we'll go out together again." Max either rode shotgun in the ATV or followed behind Garrett whenever he rode on horseback.

During the warmer weather, Max would either sleep in the barn or out on the porch, but now with the approach of winter, Garrett allowed him to bed down in the mudroom. Occasionally the dog would wander into the great room, stand in front the fireplace and look back at Garrett as if telling him to light a fire. And once he did, Max would lie on the floor and fall asleep.

He scratched the furry chocolate-and-white puppy behind the ears. "I'll be back soon. Promise," Garrett added when Max let out a low whimper.

He knew he'd spoiled the canine who had become his constant companion. It had been that way the instant he'd walked out of Happy Hearts with Max against his chest, zipped up in his jacket. Max had settled against the sheepskin lining and fallen asleep during the ride back to Garrett's home. It had taken less than a week for man and dog to become inseparable. Turning on his heel, he walked out of the cabin to his pickup.

Once behind the wheel of the Dodge Ram 2500,

he sent a text to the new office manager at Abernathy Meats to let her know he was going to the Bronco Convention Center. Seconds later, she sent him a thumbs-up and a bison emoticon that made Garrett smile. He'd never thought the company's previous office manager, Susanna Henry, would be his sister-in-law once she married his brother Dean.

It was as if the love bug had bitten all of Hutch and Hannah's sons. Widower Tyler was engaged to Callie Sheldrick and, once they were married, she would become a mother to his adorable little daughter Maeve. Even serial-dater Weston wasn't exempt—he'd fallen for Everlee "Evy" Roberts and her angelic daughter Lola. Garrett didn't want to be cynical about falling in love, but he knew from experience that it didn't always last. His adage was "been there, done that." However, he was happy his brothers had found someone with whom to share their lives and future.

So long as no one expected him to do the same.

He shifted the pickup into gear and drove away from the modern log cabin on the ranch that had become his sanctuary. Other than sitting on a horse, it was where he felt most comfortable and, within seconds of closing the door to the outside world, he relaxed, comfortable in the isolation to which he'd become accustomed. Garrett knew his mother was concerned that other than working with his brothers he was spending too much time alone. What Hannah Abernathy failed to understand was that he'd lost ten years of his life struggling to make someone else

happy while at the same time sacrificing his own happiness.

Garrett tapped a button on the steering wheel and "Blue Ain't Your Color" filled the interior of the pickup. He increased the volume as he sang along with one of his favorite country singers. After spending a decade in New York, his taste in music now alternated between country, rap and hip-hop. Beyond music, the city had exposed him to a way of life other than the one he'd known growing up on a Montana cattle ranch. One with a faster pace. Riding the bus, being packed in a subway car like a sardine, or attempting to navigate sidewalks teeming with more people in ten square blocks than in all of Bronco, was something he wouldn't ever miss. Once he'd returned to his hometown, Garrett realized the time he'd spent in New York City wasn't what he'd thought of as living. He'd only been existing in a world in which he'd never felt comfortable.

It was different with his ex-wife. Faith had taken to city life like a duck to water. She'd loved eating at different restaurants, visiting museums and art galleries, and hanging out at clubs with her new friends, while he'd preferred spending nights in their Brooklyn Heights apartment watching television.

While he hadn't begrudged Faith's newfound social life, both had known their relationship was falling apart with each passing year. One day, he'd told Faith he was going back to Bronco. She hadn't argued with him or even attempted to convince him to stay. And now, when he looked back, Garrett real-

ized she'd been relieved. The divorce was quick and amicable, and when finalized, he'd come home. This time to stay.

All too soon, the drive ended as he maneuvered into the newly remodeled convention center's parking lot.

He found the manager's office and knocked lightly on the door.

Chuck Carter swiveled in his chair and beckoned to him. "Come in, Abernathy. You're right on time. Please sit down." He motioned to the chair in front of the ornately carved mahogany desk. "I know you wanted to talk to me and the catering manager, but he's running late, so right now it's just you and me."

Removing his Stetson, Garrett folded his body onto the cushioned chair. "I don't know if you're aware that Abernathy Meats is now selling bison meat."

Chuck nodded. "There are very few things that remain a secret in Bronco."

"We've received orders from a couple of restaurants in Colorado, but I'd like to make Bronco a priority." He quickly outlined that he wanted Chuck to consider adding the burgers to the catering menu for the upcoming Mistletoe Rodeo.

"I like…" Chuck's voice trailed off when the public address system blared an announcement that the Hawkins Sisters were practicing in the arena. He stood. "You can finish telling me what you want while I go say hello to the Hawkinses."

Garrett also rose and put on his hat. He knew the convention manager had a full schedule and his as-

sistant had penciled Garrett in between meetings. He continued his presentation as they walked along a hallway that led to the arena floor.

"I like what you're offering, Abernathy," Chuck said. "Do you think you can give me something in writing, like yesterday, that I can pass along to the catering manager? I have your number, so can he call you if he has a question."

"Of course." As soon as he returned to the ranch, Garrett would go over and fine-tune the proposal he'd drawn up and then have his office manager email it to the convention manager. He'd also drafted a preliminary contract between Abernathy Meats and the Bronco Convention Center just in case.

Chuck shook his head. "I'm sorry I can't give you more time, but I promised the Hawkins Sisters I would meet with them as soon as they arrived. Having them and the Burris Brothers perform in the Mistletoe Rodeo is guaranteed to put lots of butts in the seats. We're close to a sellout."

Garrett smiled and nodded. The three-day event was certain to generate a great deal of revenue for the city.

"Have you ever met them?" Chuck asked him.

"Who?" Garrett asked.

"The Hawkins Sisters."

"No." Garrett had only watched them from the stands at the Bronco Summer Family Rodeo.

"If you have time, want an introduction?"

Garrett nodded. "I'd like that." The rodeo exploits of the Hawkins Sisters were legendary and meeting them in person was something he could brag about to his brothers.

They continued walking down a long hallway and entered a door that led directly to an area less than a hundred feet from the dirt-covered arena floor. Garrett sucked in a lungful of breath as he stared at the slim rider taking a horse through its paces around three barrels. He couldn't pull his gaze from the long dark-brown curls falling to the middle of her back and moving as if they'd taken on a life of their own as she steered the horse within inches of each barrel without tipping them over. It was as if the woman and animal were one, as if each was aware of the other's thoughts. It was only when he felt the constriction in his chest that Garrett was forced to exhale. If he'd felt most comfortable on horseback, then this woman had been born to sit a horse.

"She's magnificent."

"The horse or the woman?" Chuck asked, smiling.

He gave the man a sidelong glance. "The woman."

"That she is. That's Brynn Hawkins."

"What do you know about her?"

"All I know is that she's totally committed to her career. There was talk that the Hawkinses were thinking about establishing Bronco as their permanent residency while they tour, but you know rodeo folks can't stay in one place too long. It's always the next town, big adventure, trophy and prize money. My grandfather used to say the same thing about traveling circuses back in the day." Chuck pointed to four women standing along the fence a short distance away. "That's Brynn's mother, Josie. She's their manager. The others are Brynn's sisters, Corinne, Remi and Audrey. Just watching them perform is indeed a remarkable sight."

Garrett knew all about Audrey. She and Geoff Burris's brother Jack had competed head-to-head in the Bronco Summer Family Rodeo. The media had gone gaga over Jack Burris and Audrey Hawkins, calling them rodeo sweethearts, and there were rumors about the possibility of a movie based on their engagement. "It seems as if Audrey's put Bronco on the map with Hollywood folks following her and Jack's every move."

Chuck ran a hand across the back of his neck. "I've heard a few complaints that having a lot of media around is spoiling our quality of life, but I don't agree with them. Having hometown heroes like the Burris Brothers and the Hawkins Sisters here in Bronco spells success for everyone. Whenever they perform, they bring in out-of-town folks that are willing to patronize our local businesses."

"I agree."

The two words had just slipped off Garrett's tongue when Brynn dismounted, handed the reins to a young man and walked to where he and Chuck were standing. The other Hawkinses followed her. Seeing her this close made him aware that not only was she breathtakingly beautiful, she was also a lot younger than he'd thought. Maybe her early twenties and much too young for a man in his forties. However, that didn't stop him from staring at the light sprinkling of freckles on the pert nose and cheeks of her café au lait complexion. But it was her full lips and delightful chin with just a hint of a dimple that held him in a soporific spell from which he didn't want to escape.

Chuck smiled. "Brynn, Josie, Audrey, Corinne and Remi, I would like you to meet a fan of yours. Ladies, this is Garrett Abernathy."

"Are you here to take more photos of us?" Remi asked, prompting her mother to give her a slight nudge.

Garrett touched the brim of his hat. "Pleasure to meet you, ladies. I can assure you that I'm not a part of the media. I only wanted to meet you because I saw you perform this summer, and I thought you were spectacular."

Josie smiled. "I'm really proud of my daughters."

"You should be," Chuck said, "because it's an honor that they're going to be here for what is now our annual Mistletoe Rodeo."

"Are you involved in the rodeo?" Remi asked Garrett.

"No. I'm a rancher. My family owns Abernathy Meats and the Flying A Ranch."

"So, you're one of those Abernathys," Brynn said, speaking for the first time while meeting his eyes.

Garrett's eyebrows lifted slightly. "Should I assume you've heard of us?" There was teasing tone in his query.

A hint of a smile tilted the corners of Brynn's mouth. "One would have to live on another planet not to recognize the name. I'm of the belief that every Montanan knows about Abernathy Meats. In fact, I visited your booth during the Fourth of July barbecue."

"You must have come by when I wasn't manning the booth, and if that's the case, then you would've seen my brothers. By the way, do you eat meat or are you a vegetarian?"

Her smile grew wider. "I eat meat. I love a good rib eye, though I'm partial to a salad on occasion."

Corinne grunted under her breath. "Is it ribeye or is it bison burgers, Brynn?"

Garrett didn't miss the disapproving glance Brynn gave her sister. "It's both."

"The Abernathys are now selling bison meat," Chuck whispered as if revealing a family secret.

"You're kidding?" Audrey asked. "That's all Brynn will eat now since she had a bison burger at a restaurant in Billings last year."

Garrett angled his head. "That sounds serious."

"It is," Brynn confirmed. "The first time I ordered one, I was hooked. And then when I compared the nutritional profile of bison to beef, I decided it was worth the higher price."

"There's nothing wrong with beef," Garrett said, smiling.

Remi laughed. "Spoken like a true cattle rancher."

Garrett smiled for the first time since their introduction and Brynn noticed the attractive lines around his eyes. *He should smile more often*, she thought. The expression had replaced the sadness she'd peeked at behind his eyes, and she wondered what had happened in his life to put it there.

However, something about the rancher connected with her; something Brynn found hard to explain. To say he was handsome was an understatement. Brynn had encountered scores of men when touring the rodeo circuit and, while some flirted with her, Garrett Abernathy appeared slightly aloof. Her sisters had accused her of being overly maternal, and that was what she was feeling at the moment. Something about the rancher made her want to reach out to him.

"How would you and your family like to be our guests for the Mistletoe Rodeo?" The invitation had come out unbidden, and Brynn wondered where that had come from. "My family gets a block of premium seats we can use as we see fit."

Garrett blinked slowly. "Are you sure?"

"Yes, she's sure," Josie said, smiling. "We're doing the same for Geoff Burris's family."

Brynn knew she'd shocked Garrett with the offer. "You really would be doing us a favor because empty seats aren't a good look for the front rows."

He smiled again. "I accept your generous offer on behalf of my family. I don't know if you're aware of it, but there're a lot of Abernathys in Bronco."

Brynn's smile matched his. "The more, the merrier. I'll let the box office know to put them aside in your family's name. They'll just have to show some ID and that's it."

Garrett touched the brim of his Stetson again. "Thank you again, and it's been my pleasure to meet all of you. I'll see you at the event." He nodded to Chuck, turned on his heel and walked away.

"Wow!" Audrey whispered in Brynn's ear once Garrett was out of sight.

"What are you wowing about?" she asked Audrey.

"Garrett Abernathy. He's absolutely gorgeous."

Brynn nodded. "He is rather handsome."

Audrey draped an arm over Brynn's shoulders and pulled her out of earshot of the others. "He's beyond handsome, big sister, and what are you going to do about it?"

Brynn shrugged off the arm. "I don't know what you're talking about."

"Open your eyes, Brynn. Didn't you see how he was staring at you?"

"No. He was looking at all of us."

"Yeah right," Audrey drawled.

Corinne came over to join Brynn and Audrey. "Just because she's booed up, she expects everyone to fall in love and live happily ever after," she said facetiously.

Brynn rounded on her youngest sister. Corinne had been a funk since she and Geoff's brother had stopped talking to each other. "Just because you broke up with Mike Burris, there's no need to take your bad mood out on everyone."

"When are you going to stop acting like my mother?" Corinne said from between clenched teeth.

"When you decide to grow up and act like an adult," Brynn replied angrily. Closing her eyes, she counted slowly to ten as Corinne stomped across the floor of the arena toward an exit. Brynn couldn't help it. Whenever Josie didn't tour with them, Brynn felt she was responsible for her three younger sisters.

Audrey reached for Brynn's hand, lacing their fingers together. "You can't let her get to you, Brynn. Corinne is very emotional right now."

"Emotional I can deal with. Nasty is something I refuse to accept." She let out a sigh and pulled her hand away from Audrey's. "We're a family and we depend on one another for everything. And I mean *everything*. We're the Hawkins Sisters and that means all for one and one for all. I'm sorry that Corinne and Mike aren't speaking to each other, but she has to learn to separate her personal feelings from the professional. She must be in the right frame of mind when we compete in the Mistletoe Rodeo."

"Don't worry, Brynn. I'll talk to her. It helps that we're both involved with Burris brothers."

"Thanks." She hoped Audrey could talk to Corinne and help her deal with her on-again, off-again relationship with Mike Burris. After all, they were both involved with men who were in rodeo—a situation with which Brynn was remarkably familiar.

It had been almost two years since her last relationship, and she should've known it wouldn't end well because it had been her second meaningful relationship with a rodeo cowboy. One was fraught with jealousy and competition; the second shrouded in secrecy. There were constant arguments as to who'd earned more prize money, trophies and received the most press coverage. Brynn had vowed never again. Never again would she get involved with someone in her profession.

She was happy when Audrey and Jack Burris were able to work through their differences; they were full-time rodeo superstars and were now engaged to marry. It was different with Corinne and Mike. He was involved with the rodeo but had recently put the sport on hold to start attending medical school—something Corinne had to understand. Rodeo, for him, was only temporary.

Brynn herself wasn't certain how long she would continue to perform, but she did have a plan B. And that plan had nothing to do with her competing while astride a horse. She knew her time for competing was ending, and she had even mentioned this to her mother. As a professional rider, she'd been lucky not to have sustained any serious injuries, but the thrill of traveling from city to city and state to state was beginning to lose its allure, and she knew she had to decide in the coming year whether she could continue to compete with her sisters, or sit out some of the bookings.

She'd begun competing at the age of three in the mutton bustin' competition and then, in the junior rodeos at fifteen, winning first place in goat tying, and she'd just celebrated her sixteenth birthday when she'd begun to compete as a barrel racer. Brynn had spent most of her life as a rodeo rider and now she wondered if it was time for her to pursue another vocation—one that did not involve competing with anyone other than herself.

Chapter Two

Garrett laced his fingers together behind his head as he leaned back in the executive chair. He'd asked Dean to meet him in his office at Abernathy Meats to bring him up to date about his bison project.

Dean rapped lightly on the door before he walked in. "What's up, brother?"

Garrett sat straight. "Congratulations are in order."

"What about?" Dean asked as he sat on a chair facing Garrett.

"I just got a call from Chuck Carter over at the convention center that the caterer has put in an order for fifty pounds of bison meat for the first night of the Mistletoe Rodeo. And if he's able to sell that out, then he'll order more for the next two nights." Garrett flashed a rare smile. "You did it, Dean, when you asked Dad if we could raise bison."

Reaching over the desk, Dean gave Garrett a fist bump. "You've got that right," Dean said, grinning from ear to ear. He sobered. "I may have done the research, but you drafted the proposal and contract. So, kudos, college boy."

Garrett bit back a smirk. He'd known from an early age that he would be a rancher like his father, grandfather and great-grandfather; but he'd also wanted a solid background in business, which he'd also known would only become possible with a college degree. He'd fulfilled his wish when he'd graduated from the University of Montana in Missoula with a degree in finance.

"I saw Mom earlier this morning," Dean continued, "and she mentioned that the entire family has complimentary VIP tickets for the Mistletoe Rodeo. Is it true?"

His brother mentioning the rodeo suddenly conjured up the image of Brynn Hawkins and the cloud of soft curls falling down her back. Everything about her was so sensual that her image often popped into his head when he least expected.

"It's true. I met the Hawkins Sisters when I went to see Chuck Carter, and they invited us to attend as their guests." He'd said *they* when it was Brynn Hawkins who had issued the invitation.

Dean slapped his jeans-clad knee. "Hot damn! You must have turned on some impressive Abernathy charm for the Hawkinses to offer you comp tickets. You should use more of that mojo to find yourself a special lady to settle down with."

Garrett frowned. "Now you sound like Mom. I happen to like my life the way it is, thank you."

Dean leaned forward. "I'm only going to say this once. You're too young to shut yourself off from women."

"That's enough, Dean." There was a thread of hardness in the warning. The one thing Garrett didn't like to do was argue with his brothers. He'd been an only child for eight years until Dean was born, and since that time he worshipped his little brother and the three that had come after him. He was the big brother and had appointed himself their protector. He didn't like pulling rank and only did so when they attempted to ingratiate themselves in his personal life.

Garrett knew his defensiveness had come from his marrying and then divorcing his high school sweetheart. He'd lost count of the number of times people had remarked that he and Faith were the perfect couple. Even his parents had sung her praises. But only two of their ten years of marriage had been happy for Garrett. Faith had soured him on marriage and commitment. Even though he'd occasionally *seen* women who didn't live in Bronco following his divorce, he had made it known to them that he did not date. For him, dating was akin to a commitment, and he didn't do commitment.

Dean held up both hands. "I'm done."

He watched his brother walk out of the room, closing the door behind him.

Garrett knew he had to stop being so touchy whenever someone mentioned him and a woman in the same breath. What they didn't understand was that he'd given so much of himself to make his ex-wife happy that he had no more to give another woman. He was willing to offer friendship, but not much beyond that. And some of the women he'd met since his divorce had wanted more than friendship. They'd been looking for what his parents had, but that wasn't in the cards for him. After forty-six years of marriage, Hannah and Hutch still had what they called date night, when Hannah prepared an intimate dinner for just the two of them or Hutch took her out to a nice restaurant.

Garrett was looking forward to the rodeo and especially to watching the Hawkins Sisters compete. He didn't know why, but he wanted to see Brynn again to discover what it was about her that had made him feel an instant connection the moment their eyes met.

Garrett maneuvered into the Bronco Convention Center's parking lot and discovered there were hardly any empty parking spaces. After circling the lot twice, he decided to take advantage of valet parking. He gave the attendant the Ram's key fob, took the chit, and practically ran to the ticket window and gave the woman his name.

She smiled, drawing his attention to the ruby-red color on her lips that was the exact shade of her long, straight hair. "So, you're another one of those Abernathys. I need to see some ID."

Clearly, the rest of his family had beat him to the arena. Reaching into the front pocket of his jeans, Garrett took out the case with his driver's license. Seconds later, the woman pushed a lanyard with a plastic-covered ticket stamped "VIP" through the opening.

"Thank you."

The woman winked at him. "You're welcome, cowboy."

Garrett found the door leading to the section and row on the ticket, but before he could descend the stairs, he heard the opening notes of the national anthem and stopped. He removed the baseball cap that had seen better days, placed it over his chest, and mouthed the words to the song. A cheer went up from the assembly when the anthem ended, followed by an ear-shattering boom from the powerful sound system that seemed to shake the building's foundation. The rodeo had the energy of a rock concert with the emcee's gift for gab and the DJ playing the Rolling Stones' "Start Me Up." Garrett made his way down the steps to a row lined with family members and sat next to Tyler.

"We thought you weren't coming," Tyler said.

"I got tied up on the phone with someone from the feed company. There's no way I was going to miss this." Garrett glanced over at Callie Sheldrick, Tyler's fiancée, and smiled. She was holding Tyler's daughter, Maeve, on her lap. He marveled that the toddler was sleeping so soundly with all the noise going on around her.

He glanced down the row to see his brother Crosby, his parents, and Dean and Susanna. There was also his brother Wes, with his fiancée and her four-year-old daughter, Lola, who was Evy's mini-me with green eyes and long dark hair. Garrett waved at Lola, who smiled and shyly return the gesture. He pulled up short a moment, thinking that he was a son, brother and uncle, but not a father. He and Faith had tried to have children, but that had eluded them and, in the end, doomed their marriage when Faith admitted adoption wasn't the right choice for her.

"You made it, bro."

Garrett shifted to find that Crosby had come around to sit next to him. "Did you think I'd miss this?"

Crosby leaned closer. "Brynn Hawkins came over to introduce herself before you got here. And when she didn't see you, she asked if you were coming." He paused. "Is there something going on between the two of you?"

Garrett frowned. "No." He wanted to tell him there couldn't be anything going on between them when he'd just met Brynn a few days ago.

"If that's the case, then I thought maybe…maybe you'd talk to her about…" His words trailed off as he ducked his head.

"About you?" he asked, completing Crosby's statement. His brother nodded. "Are you saying you're interested in her?"

Crosby smiled. "That's exactly what I'm saying. In case you haven't noticed, she's beautiful."

Garrett wanted to tell Crosby he was more than

aware of Brynn's incredible beauty. Instead he said, "Chuck Carter happened to introduce me the Hawkinses and that's when Brynn invited us to be her family's guests."

"So there's nothing going on between you two?" Crosby repeated.

"Like I said, no." And he doubted there would ever be anything between them because he was so much older than Brynn. It was obvious she was closer in age to thirty-one-year-old Crosby than him.

"Thanks, bro. I'm going to get some beer. Do you want me to bring you one back?"

"Sure. And thanks."

Garrett stretched out his long legs as he settled back in his seat. He was annoyed with Crosby asking to set him up with Brynn for several reasons. First, he didn't know if she was involved with someone and, second, he'd never functioned as matchmaker for any of his siblings because he'd resented their attempts to hook *him* up with women. However, that didn't stop them from dropping poorly veiled hints. Most times, he ignored them by remaining silent. And if they persisted, he'd give them the death glare and warn them of the potential consequences of interfering in his personal life.

Maeve woke and began fidgeting, so Callie handed her to Tyler. She let out a loud shriek and held out her chubby arms to Garrett. "Hey, pretty girl," he crooned as he took the child and cradled her against his chest. Maeve yawned and settled back to sleep. Garrett dropped a light kiss on her soft curls.

"I don't know what it is about you and kids," Tyler said. "You're like a baby whisperer. The minute you walk in the room, Maeve forgets about everyone and comes over to you."

"Lola and Maeve know that I'm their favorite uncle."

"Favorite or not, you need kids of your own. Everyone says you'd be a terrific father."

A hint of a smile crinkled the skin around Garrett's eyes. "Right now, I'm enjoying being a terrific uncle. And once this little cupcake is old enough to sit on a horse, Uncle Garrett will teach her to rope and ride."

Tyler chuckled. "I don't mind her riding as long as she doesn't talk about wanting to join the rodeo circuit."

He wanted to remind his brother that Maeve was an Abernathy and growing up on the Flying A was an adventure unto itself. Garrett was five when Hutch had sat him in front of him on a horse, one arm holding him firmly while the other held the reins to the gentle mare. A slow walk became a canter and then a full gallop as the wind and the smell of freshly mowed grass had become a natural high to which he'd instantly become addicted.

"That's something you won't have to concern yourself with for a long time, Tyler."

"You're right. I have time to get ready for some snot-nosed boy coming around asking if he can date my daughter, and I'll only give him permission after I have someone conduct an intensive background check on him."

Garrett grunted and shook his head. Once men had daughters of their own, they had flashbacks of what they'd done with some other man's daughter. "Good luck with that." It was something he wouldn't have to concern himself with.

He straightened when he saw Brynn talking to a man several rows below from where he sat with his family. Garrett saw her smile when the man lowered his head to say something in her ear. She nodded before he walked away. A moment later, she turned and looked in Garrett's direction at the same time an expression of recognition flitted over her features. She climbed the stairs to his row and took the seat Crosby had vacated.

"Hello again."

His eyebrows lifted slightly. Why, Garrett asked himself, had he not realized the sultry timbre of Brynn's voice? It was low and undeniably sexy—as sexy as the woman in a pair of body-hugging jeans and as feminine as the curls flowing over the white peasant blouse embroidered with tiny blue flowers. The scent of her perfume wafted to his nostrils and it, too, was as wholly sensual as the woman wearing it.

He nodded. "Hello to you, too. Thank you again for the tickets. Although I'd planned to attend the rodeo, I know I wouldn't have been able to sit this close to the action."

Brynn glanced up at the upper deck. "It looks like a sellout."

"And probably tomorrow and the next day," Garrett added. "Are you on the program tonight?"

"No. I'm performing tomorrow in the barrel racing, tie-down calf roping, and Sunday afternoon in the steer undecorating. My sisters are competing all three days in the barrel racing, breakaway calf roping and team roping."

Garrett wanted to ask Brynn how it was to compete with her sisters in the same event and whether their relationships were fraught with sibling rivalry. Fortunately, he and his brothers weren't competitive—at least not with one another—and they were always on board whenever it came to ensuring the success of the family ranch and business.

"On behalf of my family, thank you again for the generous offer."

A hint of a smile parted Brynn's lips, bringing Garrett's gaze to linger there before it moved lower to the badge suspended from the lanyard and resting between her breasts. In that instant he'd tried imagining what Brynn would look like without her clothes, her hair falling over her naked breasts, and immediately chided himself for the licentious musing. He didn't know what was wrong with him. Even though he'd found himself physically attracted to her, Garrett knew nothing would or could come of it because of their age difference. Crosby had asked for a personal introduction, and that's what he intended to do if given the opportunity.

"I have to go. Have fun," Brynn said, breaking into his thoughts. "By the way, your niece is precious."

Garrett smiled down at Maeve. "That she is. And beautiful." It was obvious when Brynn had introduced herself to his family, Tyler had told her Maeve was his daughter.

He watched the way the denim fabric hugged Brynn's hips as she walked back to her seat. He closed his eyes, still seeing the cloud of curls framing her beautiful face. Even if Brynn was closer to his age, he knew looking for something beyond friendship wasn't for him. Besides, they came from different worlds. Her life was full of adventure. She was a celebrity, traveling from town to town, the media following her as adoring fans chanted her name, while he was perfectly content in Bronco, sitting on a horse. That's how he wanted to spend the rest of his life.

Crosby returned, handing him a cup of ice-cold beer. "I saw you talking to Brynn. Did you mention me?"

"No. I didn't have the time."

"I'm glad you didn't because I saw the way the two of you were looking at each other."

"What's that supposed to mean?" Garrett asked defensively.

Crosby touched his cup of beer to Garrett's, smiling. "Don't get your nose out of joint, bro. It's just that I see what you fail to acknowledge. Brynn likes you and you like what you see."

"You're..." His words trailed off when Crosby abruptly left to return to his seat next to their parents. *Wrong.* His brother was wrong about Brynn. She was friendly and outgoing—something necessary for a celebrity with an avid following.

"I'll take Maeve while you enjoy your beer," Tyler

said, grinning. He reached for his daughter. It was obvious he'd overheard Crosby talking about him and Brynn.

Garrett did not want to glance down several rows to watch Brynn and the man sitting on her left, but in that moment he'd believed she'd woven an invisible spell over him from which he couldn't escape. There were times when the man leaned close enough to her for their shoulders to touch, but at no time did she turn to look directly at him. It was when he'd rested an arm over her shoulders that she reached up and removed it. It was apparent he'd overstepped, and Garrett silently applauded her for establishing boundaries. There was no doubt she was in total control of what she liked and wanted.

He shifted his attention to the dancing rodeo clowns until the first event began. Bull riding. The crowd went wild when the rider was able to stay on for the requisite eight seconds. However, tonight the bulls were the winners when they bucked off rider after rider as Tom Petty's song "Free Fallin'" echoed throughout the arena.

There was lull in the action as a tractor driver leveled the dirt on the arena floor before the barrel racing competition. As the crowd noise hummed, a shrill voice rose above the din. From behind, he heard the shriek loud and clear. Someone shouting they'd spotted Bobby Stone at the back of the arena. Seconds later, other voices joined in, claiming they, too, had seen Bobby while some claimed it was his ghost.

"These so-called Bobby Stone sightings are spooking folks," Tyler said, frowning.

Garrett doubted anyone had seen Bobby Stone because, three years ago, Bobby had died suddenly while hiking in the mountains outside the city. His things had been discovered at the edge of a steep drop—even after thorough searches of the area, his body had never been found. There was further talk that the bad luck had befallen Bobby after he'd sat on the haunted bar stool at Doug's bar. Garrett recalled the rumors had escalated with Remember Bobby Stone flyers plastered around the Bronco Convention Center several months ago.

"I don't blame them," Garrett countered. "Especially after someone threw that rock through the window at Doug's."

During the July Fourth Red, White and Bronco festivities, a stone had shattered the revelry—and the glass—at Doug's bar, with a note wrapped around it reading *A Stone You Won't Forget*. Wes had reacted quickly and lunged at Evy, who'd been working at the bar, to shove her out of the way—and got hit in the shoulder for his efforts. Fortunately, it hadn't caused him severe injury. And the incident hadn't ended badly—at least not for his brother and Evy. After all, it had brought them together.

Tyler grunted under his breath. "Maybe someone is playing a sick trick to get some of those reality paranormal television programs to come film in Bronco."

Whatever it was, Garrett felt the rumors about a dead man haunting Bronco, rocks thrown through plate-glass windows, and posters plastered around the city were definitely unnerving. "Let's hope whoever is conjuring up this craziness will eventually get tired and go away."

"I hear you," Tyler drawled. "They need to quit it before someone really gets hurt."

Garrett took a long swallow of his beer when Eric Church's "Heart on Fire" blared through the arena's powerful speakers and the crowd rose as one, singing and dancing to the upbeat rocking country tune. He leaned forward, unable to take his eyes off Brynn as she danced, waved her arms, and sang along with the assembly. Everything about her was so uninhibited that he had to smile. Her image appeared on the jumbo screens around the arena and the crowd cheered even louder when she blew them a kiss.

She's a natural, Garrett thought. Everything about Brynn, from her gorgeous face and body and outgoing personality, attributed her status as a rodeo star. It was as if she lived her life by her leave, performing in various rodeos, and he likened her to a young colt let loose to run across the prairie in wild abandon, her curls blowing in the wind.

Garrett realized that if he'd never married Faith, his view of relationships would be vastly different than what it was now. And if Brynn were older—or he were younger—he knew he would consider asking her out. However, there was no guarantee she would accept, but at least he would make the attempt.

But he was also realistic enough to know they couldn't be more than friends because their lifestyles were completely opposite of each other's. He had no intention of leaving Bronco again, while she traveled around the country for the next rodeo.

Maeve started to cry and when Tyler and Callie stood to leave, Hannah offered to take her and Lola home. Garrett knew his mother always looked for a reason to babysit the two girls.

Garrett knew once his brothers were married and began starting families of their own, he couldn't count on them spending a lot of time together with him at Doug's. It wasn't as if they couldn't plan on an impromptu boys' night out, but for now it would just be him and Crosby.

He finished his beer and thought about going to the concession area to get another when the emcee announced the start of the women's barrel racing competition. Two of the Hawkins Sisters, Remi and Corinne, were in the same event. Both had high enough scores in the first round to place them in contention for top prize.

After the barrel racing, there was another intermission and he asked his brothers and their fiancées if they wanted beer and popcorn. Tyler and Wes offered to join him to bring them back. He hadn't taken more than a dozen steps when Garrett saw Brynn at the burger stand.

"Medium or well," he whispered as he walked over to stand next to her. Standing this close made him realize she was taller than he'd originally thought. Her head popped up and she smiled. Again, Garrett found himself reacting to her like a bumbling adolescent boy meeting a girl on whom he had a crush. Her smile lit up her whole face like rays of sunlight. She didn't just smile with her mouth, but also with her eyes.

"Medium-well. I wanted to order the bison burger, but I was told they've already sold out of them."

Garrett concealed a grin. The catering manager said if they sold out on the first night, then he would order more for the next two days. "I'm sorry about that. I could arrange to have some delivered to wherever you're staying."

Brynn shook her head. "That's all right. You don't have to do that."

"It's not all right, Brynn. It's the least I could do for inviting us as your guests to the Mistletoe Rodeo."

"I told you we always get a block of seats to give away to family and friends, so it was my pleasure to offer them to you."

"This is not about tit for tat, Brynn," Garrett said. He must have gotten through to her when she reached into the back pocket of her jeans and extended her cell phone.

"Give me your number and I'll let you know when and where to send it."

Garrett tapped his name and numbers into her Contacts and then handed her back the phone. "The first one is my personal number. The second is to the office at Abernathy Meats, and the third is my parents' number in case you can't reach me at the other two."

A teasing smile lifted the corners of her mouth. "My, my. Aren't you important?"

Throwing back his head, Garrett laughed loudly. "It all depends on who I'm trying to impress."

"Well, Mr. Garrett Abernathy, I'm mighty impressed."

He nodded. "And I'm mighty impressed with you, Miss Brynn Hawkins."

As soon as the words were out of his mouth, Garrett wondered if he'd crossed the line. Did she think he was coming on to her? If things were different, he would let Brynn know that he *was* interested in her. He breathed an inaudible sigh when she smiled; he hadn't offended her.

"What do you want on your burger, Miss Hawkins?" the man grilling the meat asked Brynn.

"Just grilled mushrooms."

Garrett wanted to stay and talk to Brynn but knew his brothers were waiting. "It's been nice talking to you. I'll see you tomorrow." He'd said it as if it were a foregone conclusion that they would speak again the next day.

"If not tomorrow, then Saturday. Do you plan on coming Saturday?" she asked.

"I wouldn't miss it," he confirmed. There was no way he planned to miss seeing her ride Friday night and Saturday afternoon. "My brothers are waiting for me, so we'll talk again on Saturday."

Dean met him and handed him two tubs of popcorn. "We were waiting for you to finish flirting with the pretty lady."

"I wasn't flirting with her. We were talking about bison burgers."

"Well, it sure looked like it with both of you grinning at each other like Cheshire cats."

"Let's go, Casanova," Wes joked, his blue eyes twinkling in amusement.

Garrett knew his brothers were going to tease him about Brynn until he reached the point where he would have to shut them down. As the eldest of five boys, he was the only one who had married at twenty-two and therefore hadn't earned the reputation as one of Bronco's most eligible bachelors.

He was aware that whenever a male Abernathy entered a room, their presence commanded attention—especially from the other sex. Now that three of his brothers were engaged, the pool for Hutch and Hannah's unmarried sons left only Crosby, because Garrett did not put himself in the marriageable equation. He wouldn't mind establishing a friendship with Brynn if she lived in Bronco. But a friendship with benefits was out of the question because Garrett knew if he crossed that line with her, there would be no turning back. To him, intimacy meant commitment, and that wasn't something he was willing to risk again.

Chapter Three

It was early Saturday afternoon and Brynn stood in a circle with her mother, Josie, and sisters in an area set aside for competitors and executed a group hug. The Hawkins Sisters had won prizes in each of the four categories in which they'd competed. The crowd had gone wild for Audrey, whose love story with Jack Burris had made them as well known as his superstar brother Geoff.

Josie's cell phone rang, and she dropped her arms to answer the call. "I need to take this," she said, tapping the phone icon. The skin around her brown eyes crinkled when she smiled. "Yes, thank you." She ended the call, her smile still in place. "It's confirmed. I managed to get a reservation at DJ's Deluxe for a large party at seven o'clock tonight."

A momentary look of discomfort settled into Audrey's features. "Mom, I meant to tell you that Jack invited me to have dinner with his family tonight. I'm sorry, Corinne, but Mike won't be there because he's still away school."

Josie gave Audrey a direct stare as the line of her mouth tightened in frustration. "Now you tell me."

Audrey managed to look contrite. "I'm really sorry, Mom."

The older woman closed her eyes for several seconds. "But I suppose all is not lost if the Abernathys join us. Brynn, I'd like you to invite Garrett and his family. It would be embarrassing for me to finally get the reservation and only have four of us show up."

Brynn stared wordlessly at Josie, her heart pounding a runaway rhythm against her ribs as she registered her mother's suggestion. Although she'd promised Garrett they would speak again, their talking to each other did not translate into interacting at a social gathering surrounded by their families.

She'd experienced the similar sensation at the concession stand the other night. Garrett had approached her without warning and, when she'd looked up into his deep brown eyes with lashes better suited to a woman, she'd felt something that she hadn't in a long time. There was an appeal about the way Garrett Abernathy stared at her that was mesmerizing. She'd never had another man look at her like that. It wasn't lewd or lascivious, more what she interpreted as oddly interested.

If she were honest with herself, she would admit

she was interested in Garrett and also that her thoughts about him were less than modest. Audrey was right. He was absolutely gorgeous. The lighter strands of his thick, brown, wavy hair at the temples appeared more gold than gray, and he was all cowboy in jeans, boots, whether he wore a baseball cap or a Stetson. His living and working on a cattle ranch had solidified her image of him as the quintessential modern-day cowboy.

"Okay," Brynn said breathlessly, hoping her family didn't notice she sounded less than her usual confident self. Brynn started to walk toward the entrance that led to the VIP section then quickly changed her mind, stopped, and decided to send him a text. It was a full minute before he texted back that he and his family would meet her at DJ's Deluxe later that night.

Turning on her heel, she walked back to her mother. "Garrett said the Abernathys confirm they're coming," she said to Josie. Her sisters stared at Brynn as if she'd grown a third eye. "Why are y'all looking at me?"

"You have his number?" Corinne asked.

She blinked once. "Yes. Why?"

Audrey crossed her arms under her breasts. "That was fast."

Brynn glared at Audrey. "No faster than when you hooked up with Jack Burris. And it's not like that with me and Garrett."

"What is it like?" Remi singsonged.

"Enough, girls," Josie warned in a quiet voice. "In

case you forgot, I raised y'all to be respectful of one another when it comes to your personal lives."

Brynn mouthed a thank-you to Josie. She knew her mother was overly sensitive about relationships because she'd recently separated from her husband of more than thirty years. Brynn didn't know what had happened to make her parents split up and hadn't asked. She knew Josie wouldn't tell her because she didn't want her children to take sides. Brynn loved her mother and her father and hoped there would come a time when they could work out their differences and reconcile.

She also loved her sisters, even though they all didn't share the same DNA. She and Audrey were the biological children of Josie and Steve, who'd adopted biological sisters Remi and Corinne after their horse trainer mother passed away in a tragic riding accident. Ever since that day, she'd never thought of Corinne and Remi as anything but her sisters.

Removing her hat, Audrey ran her fingers through her long black hair. "I need to get home to shampoo and blow-dry my hair before I see Jack later tonight."

Remi laughed. "I'm certain Jack has mussed up that hair a few times."

Brynn bit her lip to stop a smile as Audrey lowered her eyes. Remi loved to tease her sisters. However, it was always in wholesome fun.

"I'm also going home to unwind before tonight," Brynn said.

"Don't forget to wear something sexy for your drop-dead gorgeous cowboy," Corinne said.

"Yeah, right," Brynn drawled.

She didn't own anything sexy, but she knew for certain there were garments in her closet that were less casual than her ubiquitous jeans. And "sexy" wasn't an adjective Brynn ascribed to herself despite all the attention she got from men. She was tall, slender, and whenever she went to buy clothes, salespersons told her that she was a dressmaker's dream because whatever she tried on in her size was a perfect fit. Perfect or not, she preferred jeans to dresses and boots to stilettoes. While some women collected designer shoes and handbags, Brynn collected Western-style boots and hats.

She was also aware that it hadn't been easy for her mother to arrange for them to eat at DJ's Deluxe. When Brynn first moved to Bronco, she'd tried to get into the Bronco Heights upscale barbecue restaurant and found out reservations were necessary and that advance bookings for Saturday nights usually filled up as much as a month in advance. Whatever Josie had done or said, she applauded her mother's efforts because she was looking forward to eating there.

When her family talked about making Bronco their permanent residence, Brynn had decided she didn't want to continue to live with her sisters and had signed a lease to sublet a month-to-month basis apartment in BH247—an exclusive upscale complex in Bronco Heights—while her sisters still rented a house in the more middle-class Bronco Valley.

The living arrangements were conducive for her because she tended to take her role as the eldest a little too far at times. Brynn had grown up looking after her younger sisters and, even at thirty, she tended to be overly motherly and occasionally much too bossy.

Brynn also liked living alone because it gave her time and space to devise her plan B for life after the rodeo. Not many people knew there was the adventuresome Brynn Hawkins who never felt more alive than when riding a horse at breakneck speed around an arena or across a stretch of land. Or that there was the artistic Brynn who managed to shut out everything around her whenever she lost herself in a needlecraft project.

Josie had labeled Brynn her princess because, as a child, she'd told her mother after listening to her read her favorite fairy tales that she wanted to marry a prince and live happily ever after. She hadn't met her prince and she wasn't looking for one. Her past two relationships had dashed all hopes that she would find a man not willing to mold her into someone he wanted her to be. They'd failed to recognize that she'd come from an extensive line of strong women who were in complete control of their own destinies.

Brynn hugged her mother. "I'll meet you at DJ's Deluxe at seven."

"Wear something pretty," Josie murmured in her ear.

"Mom!"

Josie smiled. "Don't 'Mom' me and just do it."

"Okay. I will." She didn't know what her mother was thinking, but it couldn't be trying to match her up with any of the Abernathy brothers. Despite their being drop-dead gorgeous, all but two were engaged.

Crosby and Garrett were the only ones who had attended the rodeo without dates but that did not mean they weren't involved with someone.

She took off her hat and pulled the elastic band securing her ponytail. Shaking her head, a riot of curls cascaded over her shoulders and down her back. There were still a few other events on the afternoon program, but Brynn just wanted to go home and unwind. It had been an exciting three days and the Mistletoe Rodeo had surpassed its hype with the number of media in attendance. Bronco had to thank hometown rodeo hero Geoff Burris for making it an annual event.

Brynn left the convention center and walked to the section of the lot where she'd parked her recently purchased Jeep Gladiator. She'd put so many miles on her last vehicle that she'd doubted it would survive the frigid Montana winter.

As soon as she sat behind the wheel, the excitement of the past three days dissipated much like letting the air out of a balloon. Lately, it was as if she had to engage in mental calisthenics to psych herself up for the competitions. Much like a Super Bowl MVP who announced they were going to Disneyland or Disney World, Brynn wanted to go to the Florida Keys to sip cocktails, overindulge on seafood, watch the gorgeous sunsets, and then fall asleep to the sounds of the breeze rustling palm fronds and the incessant croaking of frogs.

Next year, she thought. She wasn't certain about all of the events Josie had on the calendar for the following year, but Brynn promised herself that after performing in any two-day rodeo she was going to go away for a week to decompress.

Garrett took the good-natured ribbing from family members in stride when they said his flirting with Brynn was the reason she'd extended an invitation to join the Hawkinses for a celebratory dinner. He knew trying to convince them he hadn't been flirting was futile, so he decided to save his breath. Besides, when Brynn had sent him the text, she had indicated it was her mother's request.

Garrett arrived at the restaurant at the same time Hutch was assisting Hannah out of his vehicle.

His mother's eyebrow lifted slightly when she gave him the once-over. "I'm glad you decided not to wear that confounded corduroy jacket tonight."

Garrett dropped a kiss on his mother's cheek. "I don't know why my jacket bothers you so much."

Hannah reached for his hand. "It's just that I've come to think of it as somewhat of a security blanket for you. That you don't feel in control unless you're wearing it."

He glanced over at Hutch, who'd shrugged his shoulders, and knew his father wasn't about to offer his opinion. "The same can be said whenever I wear a Stetson or a baseball cap. How often do you see me go bareheaded?"

A beat passed. "You've got me there," Hannah admitted.

Garrett didn't want to get into a debate with his mother about his wardrobe. He didn't know why he was superstitious, but the jacket had become his go-to garment, much like his Stetsons or favorite baseball caps, making him feel as if he was truly home. Tonight, because he was dining at DJ's Deluxe, he'd opted for a pair of dark gray tailored slacks, a white shirt with a banded collar, a navy blue jacket, and black leather low-heeled boots. He opened the door to the restaurant, allowing his parents to enter before he gave the hostess his name and she instructed someone to show them where the Hawkins had gathered.

It had taken Garrett at least five seconds to recognize Brynn. She'd swept the curls off her face and shoulders and had fashioned them into a twist on the nape of her slender neck. A white silk blouse tucked into the waistband of a long black suede skirt covered the tops of a pair of matching boots. A wide zebra-print belt showed off a narrow waist he could span with both hands. Her lips parted in a friendly smile and Garrett acknowledged it with one of his own.

"You look incredible." Brynn lowered her eyes, and he'd found himself mesmerized by the demure gesture.

"Thank you. You clean up quite well yourself."

He inclined his head. Did she like seeing him dressed down in jeans and his favorite jacket or did she prefer him wearing tailored clothes? Garrett knew his ex-wife's preference. Faith had turned into a fashion critic whenever they'd go out together, selecting what she wanted him to wear because she claimed she didn't want him to embarrass her when they socialized with her hoity-toity New York City friends.

The few times he'd reminded her that he was aware of what was appropriate for different venues ended with her storming out of their apartment without him. Her friends had never become his, and during the years he'd lived there, Garrett had felt more like an escort than a husband. He could not believe how a small-town country girl had transformed herself into a cosmopolitan sophisticate within six months of their relocating from Montana.

Brynn leaned closer, close enough for him to inhale the scent of coconut clinging to her hair. "I miss seeing you in your corduroy jacket."

"You like it?" Garrett asked, not knowing why her opinion would mean that much to him.

"Yes. I have a few in assorted colors."

He chuckled. "I suppose that makes us kindred spirits."

In that instant, Garrett vowed not to compare Brynn to Faith, as he had with every woman he'd met since his divorce, because he knew it wouldn't be fair to her. Brynn was Brynn and Faith was Faith, and they were as different from each other as day from night, both in personality and physical appearance.

Garrett noticed Josie's approach. And as much as he wanted to continue talking to Brynn, he saw that everyone had taken their seats at the round table. Maeve was in a highchair flanked by Tyler and Callie, while Lola, in a booster seat, sat between Wes and Evy.

"My mother is pedantic when it comes to starting on time," Brynn whispered. "So let's join the others."

Resting his hand at the small of Brynn's back, Garrett steered her to the table. The first thing he noticed were the place cards, and that he and Brynn were to sit together. "Place cards?"

Brynn nodded. "That's something my mother insists on whenever we eat with a large group of people."

Josie smiled. "My daughters know that I'm an organizational person, so that's why I decided on place cards. It will make it easier for the servers to take your menu selections. There will be unlimited wine, beer and pop for everyone, so order whatever you want and please enjoy."

"Your mother must also have exceptional negotiating proficiency to land a reservation for a party this large on a Saturday night," he said to Brynn. He'd said that although he really wanted to tell Brynn that he'd wanted to thank her mother for seating them next to each other.

Garrett pulled out a chair, seating Brynn, before sitting next to her. He glanced around the table to find Crosby sitting between Corinne and Remi. Crosby's grin indicated he was pleased with his seating arrangement. A bright flush suffused Susanna's face as Dean whispered in her ear. Garrett didn't know how Josie had known to position everyone where they were, but he was more than pleased with her organizational skills.

Brynn gave Garrett a sidelong glance and smiled. She hadn't lied to when she'd told him he cleaned up well. The first time she'd met him, he'd been clean-shaven, but when she'd encountered him again, he'd affected a stubble that had blatantly enhanced his masculinity. To be honest, she found him eye-catching either way.

"My mother has outstanding communication skills. Once she retired from the rodeo circuit, she became our manager. She has developed the innate ability to read a contract as well as any lawyer when booking the Hawkins Sisters."

"So, you and your sisters are second-generation Hawkins Sisters?"

Brynn nodded. "Actually, my grandmother had made a name for herself as a rodeo star. Seventy-something Hattie Hawkins is outspoken and one of a kind."

"Like her granddaughter?" he teased, smiling.

"No. Well, sometimes," she added. "My grandmother was in her early thirties when she joined the newly formed Women's Professional Rodeo Association. Nowadays, most members of the WPRA compete in the Professional Rodeo Cowboys Association because the purses are larger."

"After watching you and your sisters perform, I must admit you've surpassed the hype. Now that Audrey is engaged to Jack Burris, there's no doubt they will be touted as a rodeo royal couple."

Brynn agreed with Garrett's assessment of Audrey and Jack. Geoff Burris had earned the reputation as the Tiger Woods of the rodeo circuit and there was no doubt the Hawkins' and Burris' names would be on everyone's tongue once the two rodeo families were united.

"They do make quite a pair."

Shifting slightly, Garrett gave Brynn a direct stare. "Why does it sound as if you don't approve of her marrying a Burris?"

"Audrey is an adult, and she doesn't need my approval. I love her dearly and support her decision to marry Jack."

The seconds ticked before Garrett said, "There are single Burris brothers other than Jack and Geoff. Would you consider having a relationship with any of them?"

Brynn paused, wondering if Garrett had been reading her mind. "No. Been there, done that."

"Are you saying that you were once involved with a Burris?"

"No," she quickly denied. "A rodeo cowboy." She wanted to tell Garret it was with more than one rodeo rider. "And I decided that's something I don't plan to relive. I'm on compete mode once I enter the arena and turn it off after I leave it."

"Working in the same profession as your significant other can have its disadvantages."

"Are you speaking from experience, Garrett?"

"No. Thankfully, I didn't—and don't—have that problem."

"Good for you."

It was the last thing Brynn said before the servers came and asked for her dining selection, as a quartet of servers poured drinks. Josie stood and held up her glass of red wine. "I'd like to thank everyone for coming tonight and I raise my glass to toast to family and good health."

"Cheers!" everyone chanted as they touched glasses.

"To friendship," Garrett said as he clinked his beer mug with Brynn's wineglass.

She smiled and nodded. "Friendship and good health."

The gathering became more festive by the time appetizers were set on the table, and it reminded Brynn of the times when she and her sisters got together with their aunts and cousins. There was nonstop talking, eating and drinking. Brynn felt as if she'd known the Abernathys for much longer than a few days. They were friendly, unpretentious, and fun-loving.

Brynn speared a stuffed mushroom and placed it on a small dish at her place setting. She cut into it and popped a piece into her mouth as an explosion of flavors of diced onion, garlic, red and green pepper, and ham tantalized her palate. "This is so good," she said, touching her napkin to the corners of her mouth.

Garrett chewed and swallowed a mouthful of shrimp with Asian chili sauce. "I think this is better than your mushroom."

Brynn pointed with her fork to the uneaten portion on her plate. "Try it."

"I'm not particularly fond of mushrooms, but what you should try is the shrimp." He cut a piece, dipped it in the spicy sauce and extended the fork to Brynn. She opened her mouth and Garrett fed her, unaware that those sitting around the table were watching them.

"That is delicious," she said, smiling.

"I told you," Garrett said boastfully. "Even though I'm a cattle rancher, I really like seafood."

"Before I moved to Bronco, I was told there are some lakes and rivers not too far away from here where folks go fly-fishing for trout."

Garrett paused, taking another bite of shrimp. "You fly-fish?"

Smiling, Brynn nodded. "Yes. I've done it a few times and caught several trout, but I threw them back because they were too small. Do you fish?"

"Yes. A couple hours' drive north of the ranch, there's a lake teeming with trout. I managed to catch a few and cleaned them on the spot before I came home and put them in the freezer. Whenever the weather is warm, I fire up the gas grill and invite everyone over for fish."

A mysterious smile touched the corners of her mouth. "So, the cowboy cooks."

Garrett also smiled. "This cowboy grills. There is a distinct difference."

Brynn reached over and cut off a piece of shrimp from his plate. "Who taught you to grill?"

"The internet and cooking shows."

Her eyebrows lifted. "You learned watching television?"

"Yup."

"Are you any good?"

"That all depends on who's eating my cooking. So far, no one has ever said they're not coming back.

What about you, Brynn? Do you cook or just make reservations?"

Brynn's jaw dropped as she gave him an incredulous look. "You know that sounds sexist."

Instantly, Garrett knew he'd made a serious faux pas. He cursed inwardly, not understanding why he had a tendency to get in his own way every time he felt a stab of attraction for a beautiful—and accomplished—woman. He knew damn well that he owed Brynn Hawkins an apology, and fast. "I'm sorry. I honestly didn't mean to put my foot in my mouth like that. I just thought that with your touring schedule, you may not get the chance to cook for yourself."

Brynn rested a hand over his. "Apology accepted. I do cook, and very well."

"Who taught you?" He'd asked the same question she'd just asked him.

"My grandmother. One of these days, I'll tell you all about Hattie Hawkins, who really made a name for herself in the rodeo circuit back in the day."

"That's something I'm really looking forward to," Garrett said truthfully. Brynn intrigued him as no other woman had and he wanted to learn as much about her as he could before she left Bronco for another competition. "Even though I'm not a fan of mushrooms, I'm going to be a good sport and try yours."

Brynn rested a hand on his shoulder. "Spoken like a man willing to take risks."

"I'm really not that much of a risk-taker."

She cut off a piece of mushroom. "The fact that

you're willing to try it says you are," Brynn said as she fed him. "What do you think?"

He nodded after chewing and swallowing. "It's really good. Thank you."

"For what?"

"For introducing me to something new."

"Uncle Rhett, are you a baby?" Lola asked, a slight frown forming between her green eyes.

Garrett smiled across the table at Everlee's daughter. "No, I'm not. Why?"

"Why is the lady feeding you?"

There was complete silence around the table as everyone stared at him and Brynn. He hadn't given it a thought that he and Brynn were eating off each other's forks.

"Busted," Wes mumbled under his breath.

Garrett wasn't embarrassed for himself, but he hadn't wanted to put Brynn on the spot. He gave her a sidelong glance and noticed a rush of color suffusing her golden-brown complexion as she sipped from a glass of rosé.

"Miss Brynn wanted me to taste something that I thought I wouldn't like."

"Did you like it, Uncle Rhett?"

He smiled at the sassy little girl who had stolen the hearts of every Abernathy. His in particular. "I liked it a lot."

"Goodie," Lola said as she went back to munching on a breadstick.

Garrett watched as Crosby pushed back his chair and approached Hannah, who nodded and smiled. He returned to take his seat between Corinne and Remi, a smug expression on his face.

"I was just informed that the Hawkinses plan to be in Bronco through Thanksgiving. So, we would like to return the Hawkins Sisters generosity and invite them to join us at the Flying A for Thanksgiving dinner—if you all don't have any other plans, that is."

Garrett stared at his mother, stunned. He'd believed Brynn and her family would be in Bronco for a few days or no more than a week before leaving to compete in another rodeo. He'd likened the woman sitting beside him to an addictive substance. The more he saw her, the more he found himself drawn to her, and the result would be dire consequences because Garrett knew he was too old to become involved with her.

Still, he asked her, "What do you think?"

She flashed a bright smile. "I'll have to check with the others to see what they've planned, but it sounds like a lovely idea."

"So, you plan to come?"

"Speaking for myself, yes."

Garrett had been drinking beer, but at the moment he realized he needed something stronger to temporarily dull his senses since he didn't want to think of running into Brynn during her stay in Bronco. He liked her. Liked her much more than he should.

Buck up. You're a grown-ass man and a little slip of a woman shouldn't have you scared or running in the opposite direction. All you have to do is make sure what you have with her doesn't go beyond friendship.

Garrett ran a hand over his face. His inner voice

was right. He was a man with enough experience with women to control where he'd wanted a relationship to go. And now he realized what his mother had been preaching to him. He was spending too much time without female companionship. There was no reason he couldn't form a friendship with a woman who lived in Bronco without it leading to a committed relationship. A lot of men had women friends. Then again, maybe he was projecting because, with the few interactions they'd had, nothing about Brynn had indicated she wanted anything that surpassed friendship.

Check your ego, Garrett Abernathy.

Chapter Four

Brynn could not remember when she'd spent a more enjoyable time with a large group of people than she had with the Abernathys. Even Corinne seemed to have come out of her funk. She'd laughed with abandon as she and Remi intently engaged in conversation with Crosby.

"No thank you," Brynn said to the server as he attempted to refill her half-full wineglass.

"You didn't drink much," Garrett whispered in her ear.

She gave him a sidelong glance. "I'd probably finish the glass if I wasn't driving."

He angled his head, giving her a direct stare when she turned to look at him. "Can't one of your sisters drive your vehicle back home?"

"No, because my sisters and I don't live together."

"Oh? Where do you live?"

"Bronco Heights. I'm subletting an apartment month-to-month at BH247, and my sisters are renting a house in Bronco Valley. I haven't actually lived with my sisters in over five years. When we first moved to Bronco, I did stay with them in the rental for a while until my application with BH247 was approved. Competing together is altogether different from living together. More than a couple of women living under one roof is not conducive for inseparability."

"It shouldn't be any different from five men living under one roof," Garrett countered.

"I doubt if you and your brothers got into squabbles over clothes. Besides, I'm also the oldest and my sisters prefer not to live with me because they claim I'm too bossy."

Garrett leaned closer. "Are you?"

She averted her eyes at the same time she stilled when Garrett tucked a curl that had escape the bun behind her ear. "No. Just outspoken."

He dropped his hand and laughed. "And that translates into you being bossy."

"It's more like being maternal," Brynn said in defense of her dominance in the birth order.

"I'm also the eldest and I'm definitely not paternal when it comes to my brothers."

"So, you don't order them around?"

"Not as adults."

"How's your steak?" Tyler asked her.

Brynn shifted her attention from Garrett to Tyler,

sitting to her right, and met his blue eyes. The resemblance between the Abernathy brothers was obvious; it was hard to determine which one was more handsome.

"It's delicious." And it was. The aged rib eye, topped with garlic and horseradish butter, was tender and flavorful. "I can see why there's a wait list for reservations."

"You must eat in a lot of upscale restaurants when you're on the rodeo circuit."

"Some upscale and many not," she told Tyler.

"Which do you prefer?"

Brynn wondered if Tyler was feeling her out to assess whether there was the possibility of something happening between her and Garrett. And if that were the case, then she wanted to reassure him she wasn't looking for a relationship with any man. Not as long as she was still involved with the rodeo. Long-distance liaisons couldn't be successful.

"I don't judge a restaurant by Michelin stars or extravagant menu prices. I'm only there for the good food. Based on this steak, I do like this place."

"Have you tried other restaurants in Bronco?"

Tyler had asked Brynn yet another question that was beginning to feel like an inquisition. She mentioned a couple places then said, "I'm planning to eat at the Library, because my sisters have been raving about that place."

Tyler nodded. "It was an actual library before Camilla Sanchez turned it into a restaurant."

"I like what I've seen of Bronco since moving here."

"So, it's true. You actually plan to make Bronco your permanent home when you're not touring?"

"I'm still thinking about it." Brynn knew for certain Audrey would settle down in Bronco once she married Jack.

"We hope you don't take too long to think about it. Folks will never stop bragging that we have two superstar rodeo families living in Bronco."

Garrett felt like an interloper, eavesdropping on Tyler's conversation with Brynn. Chuck Carter had mentioned the Hawkinses were considering living permanently in Bronco, but Brynn had just told Tyler that she was thinking about it, and while she'd admitted to enjoying living in Bronco, Garrett knew he would run into her on a number of occasions.

Josie had asked if anyone wanted dessert, and she was met with a chorus of declinations before she signed the check and thanked the server.

"Thanks again for joining me and the family," she said. "We're all looking forward to sharing Thanksgiving with you."

Garrett pushed back his chair and then assisted Brynn. "I'll need your apartment number to deliver the bison burgers."

She smiled up at him. "I'll text you and let you know when I'll be home to receive them. And thank you again for offering."

"Are you kidding? It's the least I could do after

your family's generosity with VIP tickets to the rodeo and now dinner."

"It's a Hawkins' tradition we occasionally offer to friends and family," Brynn said, reminding him of her mother's toast.

"Speaking of traditions… You'll get to meet some of my cousins when you join us for Thanksgiving. There are a lot of Abernathys in Bronco, so I want to warn you in advance that when we're together, it can be a little overwhelming."

Brynn's smile was dazzling. "I'm looking forward to it."

Garrett stared at her straight white teeth. "I'm certain we'll get to see each other before then."

"Bronco isn't that big that we won't occasionally run into each other."

Garrett nodded. "You're right."

A beat passed. "Good night, Garrett."

He wanted to give her the obligatory hug that Crosby was exchanging with Corinne and Remi. Instead, he merely nodded and said, "Good night, Brynn."

Garrett carried Maeve as they exited the restaurant just as Tyler pulling up in front. He handed Maeve to Callie and said good night.

The temperature had dropped at least ten degrees and although the calendar indicated at least six weeks before the solstice, it felt as if winter had come early to Big Sky Country. The fall and winter were his favorite seasons, and he found every excuse to spend as much as time as he could outdoors. He'd recently purchased several portable liquid-propane patio heaters to offset the below-freezing temperatures when grilling outdoors.

He smiled when he'd recalled telling Brynn that he didn't cook but grilled, and he wondered what she would've thought if he'd invited her to his home to witness his grilling prowess, then remind himself that, other than his mother, future sisters-in-law and female cousins, he'd never invited any woman to his home. And if he and Brynn were to become friends, he still didn't know if that would ever become a possibility.

Garrett got into his pickup and maneuvered out of the parking lot, thinking about how much he'd enjoyed spending a couple of hours with the most delightful woman he'd ever met.

Flurries were falling as he pulled into the attached three-car garage and tapped the remote device on the visor to close the door. Max came to greet him as he entered the mudroom and removed his boots. "Do you want to go out?" he asked. The border collie responded with a loud bark. The dog followed him through the open floor plan to the front door, raced down the porch steps and disappeared into the darkness of the night.

Garrett knew Max would do his business and stay out long enough for him to change his clothes. Ten minutes later, he stood on the wraparound porch in a pair of jeans and running shoes, waiting for the dog to return. There were nights when Max slept in the heated barn with the horses but not tonight. The flurries had increased in intensity and there was no doubt several inches of snow would blanket the countryside before sunrise.

He saw a flash of brown and white in the glow of the porch's solar lights and smiled. His pet was back.

"Come inside, boy, where it's warm."

Max shook himself, ambled inside, and settled down in front of the stone fireplace. Garrett placed several logs and kindling on the grate. With a flick of the fire starter, the kindling caught and, within minutes, the aroma of burning wood wafted through the first story. He replaced the screen and turned off all the lights except two lamps.

"Good night, buddy," Garrett said quietly. Max may have been ready to turn in for the night, but it was still too early for him. He climbed the staircase to the second floor, walked into his bedroom suite, and flopped down on a love seat in the expansive sitting area. It had taken him more than six years to save enough money to build the home he'd always wanted. Fortunately, he hadn't had to buy the land because it was on Abernathy property and far enough from the main house and those belonging to his siblings.

Reaching for the remote on a side table, he turned on the wall-mounted television and began channel surfing until he found a basketball game. Watching television kept him from thinking about Brynn and why he wanted to see her again. Twenty minutes later his lids grew heavy. Then he changed, finished readying in the en suite bathroom, and went to bed. He fell asleep within minutes of his head touching the pillow.

Garrett woke at dawn and let Max out before he showered and pulled on a pair of threadbare jeans, a white T-shirt and thick, white, cotton socks. Surprisingly, there was less than an inch of snow on the ground and he predicted that would disappear by midmorning. It was Sunday and he planned to spend the day riding his favorite horse to check on the bison before grooming Tecumseh. He'd named the spirited Appaloosa after the famed Shawnee chief and warrior who'd formed a Native American confederacy promoting intertribal unity.

He was filling the basket in the coffee maker with grounds when the doorbell rang. Garrett glanced at the clock on the oven. It was after seven and he knew instinctively who it was. Smiling, he walked to the door and opened it.

"Good morning, sunshine," he said in greeting as his mother headed for the kitchen.

"I made your favorite muffins this morning."

"And I was just putting up a pot of coffee. So, are you going to join me?"

Hannah set the covered plastic container on the breakfast island. "Of course. I know you get up with the chickens, and because I was also up early, I decided to do a little baking."

Garrett wanted to tell his mother she was always doing a little baking. In fact, she'd felt most at home in the kitchen after raising five rambunctious sons. "Did you enjoy yourself last night?"

Hannah sat on a stool at the breakfast island. "That's what I was going to ask you."

Garrett filled the coffee maker with water and selected the brewing cycle. "Yes, I did."

"Was it because of Brynn Hawkins?"

He turned and met his mother's eyes. Had she asked and expected him to lie? "It was because of a lot of things, Mom. I happen to like the food and service at DJ's Deluxe and getting together with the family is something I always enjoy. Celebrating with the Hawkinses was definitely a bonus."

"I'm not talking about the family or the Hawkinses, Garrett. I'm referring to one Hawkins in particular."

Resting his hip against the countertop and crossing his feet at the ankles, Garrett folded his arms over his chest. "What 'one Hawkins in particular'?"

"Brynn. Do you like her?"

His impassive expression did not change. "Yes, I like her."

Hannah smiled and expelled an audible sigh. "I'm glad, because I like her, too. She's good for you, Garrett."

"Why would you say that?"

"Because you seem like a different person around her. You were doing a lot of talking and laughing, and that's something I haven't seen you do enough of since you moved back from New York."

"That's because she's easy to talk to. She's approachable and not judgmental."

"In other words, she brings out the best in you. Even your father noticed that."

Garrett threw up both hands in frustration. He knew his parents, his mother in particular, wanted to see him married again, but it wasn't what he wanted. He was content with his life and his rightful place among several generations of Abernathys. "You've been wanting me to find someone to settle down with, but that's not going to happen. Been there, done that. And definitely not with a woman who is much too young for me."

Hannah blinked slowly. "Are you talking about Brynn?"

"Yes, Mom. Brynn."

Throwing back her head, Hannah laughed uncontrollably. "You're talking about her as if she were a girl," she said once she recovered from her laughing jag. "Brynn Hawkins is a thirty-year-old woman who has been living on her own for years."

I can't believe she's thirty, Garrett thought. To him, she looked much younger. But then, he didn't know how a thirty-year-old woman was supposed to look. "She's still too young for me," he repeated.

"Oh, for heaven's sake, Garrett. There's only a thirteen year difference between the two of you."

"I would still prefer a woman closer to my age."

"And if I were to introduce you to a woman closer to your age, would you date her?"

The distinct aroma of brewing coffee filled the kitchen and Garrett turned to take down two delicate hand-painted cups, saucers and dessert plates from an overhead cabinet. The chinaware had been a gift from his parents once he'd moved into the large log cabin during what had become an informal house-warming. He never used them when eating alone, but he used them whenever his mother came over, to demonstrate how much he appreciated her generosity.

"Probably not."

"So, there goes your excuse not to date Miss Hawkins."

"I've told you over and over that I don't date."

"You don't date, yet you do see women."

Garrett reached for a trivet and set the coffee carafe on it on the countertop, then chinaware and spoons. Yes, he did see women, but it wasn't something he advertised to anyone. Especially to members of his family.

"Why would you say that?"

"Max," Hannah said, flashing a knowing grin.

"What about Max?"

"Whenever you're away overnight or even a day or two he comes around looking to be fed."

"Max lives on the ranch, and everyone feeds him."

"Max is *your* dog, Garrett, and you're the one he goes to for food. He'll only come to the main house when you're away. You're an adult, so I have no right to question your whereabouts, and I'm more than aware when my sons don't come back to the ranch that they're occupied with other things."

"Don't you mean other people?"

Hannah removed the top to the container and

placed a muffin on each dish. "I shouldn't have to spell it out for you."

After removing a small carton of cream from the fridge, Garrett sat on a stool beside his mother. He filled her cup with the steaming brew, and then his own. "You have three sons that are engaged to be married and two granddaughters. And then there's Crosby, who no doubt will be next to put a ring on a woman's finger, so there's no need for me to repeat something I suck at."

Hannah added a generous dollop of cream to her coffee and slowly stirred it as she met Garrett's eyes. "I can't believe you're blaming yourself because your marriage didn't work out. You tried to give Faith everything she'd ever wanted, and it still wasn't enough."

"Faith wanted a baby and when she couldn't have one, she decided on a lifestyle that was totally opposed to what I wanted. In the end, we were going in different directions, and that's when I decided I had to come home."

"You loved Faith more than she loved you."

Garrett took a bite of the apple strudel-filled muffin. He chewed and swallowed it, and then took a sip of strong black coffee. He didn't totally agree with Hannah. "I believe at one time that she did love me."

"She loved what you represented, and that meant what you could give her. Faith is a social climber and all she ever cared about was landing a rich husband. It didn't matter if that man was a Taylor, Abernathy, Dalton, or even a John. And when you brought her home to meet us, I knew within seconds that she wasn't right for you."

"Why didn't you say something, Mom?"

"Would you have believed me if I had said something? No," Hannah said, answering her own question. "I knew you were head-over-heels in love with her and, because you were so happy, I didn't want to do or say anything to interfere with that. I did applaud you when you told her you wanted to wait until after you graduated college to get married. And instinct told me if you hadn't given her a ring at prom, she wouldn't have waited for you."

Faith did wait. And, three weeks following his college graduation, and at the age of twenty-two, they were married at All Saints Church. The reception, hosted at The Association, a private cattleman's club for local ranchers, had all the bells and whistles of a celebrity wedding.

"That's the past and I try not to think about it," Garrett said after a comfortable silence.

"It may be the past, but you're still not over it. Meanwhile, Faith has moved on and she is now the third wife of a much-older, real-estate developer, who made her sign a prenup. Word is she sent her mother photos of her penthouse apartment overlooking Central Park."

Garrett went still. "How do you know this?"

"During my last luncheon with some of the other ranchers' wives, her name came up. I know they were waiting for me to make a comment, but I just sat there and said nothing. They didn't realize I was glad you don't have to deal with her anymore."

"I hope she's happy."

Hannah made a sucking sound with her tongue and teeth. "Women like Faith are never happy, no matter what they're given."

Garrett knew his mother was right. He'd tried to give Faith whatever she'd asked for and, in the end, it hadn't been enough. And Hannah was also right about him not getting past whatever he'd experienced in his marriage, while he didn't know why he'd felt an instantaneous connection with Brynn when that had never happened with any other woman.

"I still wish her the best."

"That's because you were never one to hold a grudge. When folks ask me who's my favorite son, I tell them I don't have one. But, if I were truthful, I'd have to say you are because, after you were born, it took Hutch and me almost eight years of trying over and over to have another baby. Even if we were only going to be blessed with one child, then that meant he was incredibly special."

Garrett chuckled. "I didn't stay incredibly special long when you had Dean, and then Weston, Crosby, and finally Tyler. What made you decide to stop with Tyler?"

She grinned. "I'd given up all hope that I would have a girl, so I got used to five boys tracking dirt over my clean floors and drinking milk and juice from the containers rather than a glass."

"I guess we were a handful when we were kids."

She rolled her eyes and laughed. "It only got worse. You were off at college by the time your brothers started noticing girls. The phone never stopped ringing and the girls never stopped calling. After a while, I'd say give me your name and I'll take a message. It finally stopped once they had their cell phones."

"I'm glad I missed that," Garrett joked. He could just imagine his mother's frustration trying to figure out who was dating which son.

"You know, I kind of miss it too." She reached out her hand and patted his. Her expression turned serious. "Raising five sons? I wouldn't have wanted it any other way."

He smiled at her. "Love you, too, Mom."

She pulled her fuzzy sweater around her. "I'm going back now to fix breakfast for your father. Are you coming over later for Sunday dinner, or do you have other plans?"

Garrett leaned over and pressed a kiss on his mother's hair. "I'll see you later. And thank you for the muffins." He was shocked when he saw Hannah's eyes fill with tears. "What's the matter, Mom?"

She blinked them back before they fell. "It's nothing."

"You never cry for nothing." It was on a rare occasion he witnessed his mother crying. The last time was when Tyler buried Luanne; not only had his brother grieved the loss of his wife, but he'd had to take care of his three-month-old baby girl. Hannah had helped Tyler with Maeve, but most times he'd insisted on taking on the full responsibility of raising his daughter.

Hannah sniffled, reached into one of the large pockets on the sweater and took out a tissue. She touched it to her nose. "I get a little weepy every once in a while. And it's not because I'm unhappy. I think back to the time when I met and fell in love with your father, and all we've been through together, and it can be a little bit overwhelming. We have this ranch, five incredible sons, and now grandchildren."

Garrett hugged her. "All's well that ends well."

Hannah blew her nose. "You're right. Now I must be going, or Hutch will think I'm out with another man."

"Yeah. One of his sons." He walked her to the door. Ducking his head, he kissed her cheek. "I'll see you later."

He waited until Hannah got into the battered pickup and drove off. He knew she was still worried about him, but there was nothing he could say to assuage her concern or convince her that he was living his best life. Not only did he love living on the Flying A, he also enjoyed helping his brothers maintain the ranch and run the family business.

And he didn't need a wife as much as he needed a woman he could relate to as a friend. Garrett smiled when he thought about Brynn Hawkins. She would be perfect because she did make him laugh—something he didn't do often enough. If she was amenable to becoming friends, then he was more than willing to agree to the arrangement.

Chapter Five

The bell chimed throughout the apartment and Brynn crossed the room to answer the door. She'd sent Garrett a text earlier that morning to let him know she would be available to receive the bison burgers Tuesday afternoon at four, and he'd returned her text that someone from Abernathy Meats would deliver them to her at that time.

She opened the door and her jaw dropped when she saw Garrett cradling a large Styrofoam cooler against his broad chest. "You!" The single word was a breathless whisper. She hadn't expected him to personally bring the burgers.

Garrett wiped his booted feet on the thick straw mat outside the door. "May I come in?"

Brynn reacted quickly, opening the door wider,

and he walked in. Although it had only been a few days since they'd last seen each other, it was like she was seeing him for the first time. Not only did he appear taller, but his shoulders seemed even broader in the brown corduroy jacket he'd put on over a black waffle-weave T-shirt.

"You startled me, because I hadn't expected you to make a personal delivery." She extended an arm. "Welcome to my humble abode."

Garrett smiled. "It doesn't look very humble to me."

"I'm still in the process of decorating it."

She'd decided to sublet the apartment in the exclusive upscale complex in Bronco Heights because of a number of onsite amenities that included indoor and outdoor pools and a hot tub.

The apartment had become a place where she was able to shed the persona of rodeo rider and just be her true self. It was where she had come to value her privacy and indulge in her crafts, and there were times when she did lose track of time sewing, knitting, crocheting and weaving. Although she loved her sisters, and there wasn't anything she wouldn't do for them, at thirty she preferred living on her own.

"You have an exquisite eye for colors," Garrett said as he walked through the entryway with its glass-covered, bleached-pine table lined with photographs, decorative candles and pots of green and flowering plants and into the living room where Brynn had chosen a sofa and matching love seat in a pale green color. Throw pillows in varying shades of purple were the perfect contrast to the calming green.

"Thank you. Come with me to the kitchen so I can see what goodies you brought."

He didn't have time to examine the dining area when he followed Brynn to the kitchen. He'd tried unsuccessfully not to stare at her slim hips blatantly outlined in body-hugging jeans, and swallowed a groan of frustration when his body refused to follow the dictates of his brain. There was something so intoxicatingly uninhibited about Brynn with her unbound hair flowing down her back that all he could think of was her naked in his bed and a riot of curls spilling over the pillow under her head. He knew if he didn't get a grip on his reaction to Brynn he would ruin any chance of them becoming friends.

"I brought you a little more than bison burgers."

Brynn turned to meet his eyes as a slight smile tilted the corners of her mouth. "What else?"

He set the cooler down. "Steaks, beef ribs, roast beef, London broil, prime rib, brisket, sausage, hot dogs, ground beef, and oxtail. All compliments of Abernathy Meats."

Brynn shook her head. "Thank you, Garrett. I'll share it with my sisters."

"There's no need for that, because I instructed someone from the warehouse to deliver a case of meat to your sisters' place in Bronco Valley. We Abernathys appreciate your family's generosity, so this is our way of saying thank you."

"I do thank you, but there's no way for me to eat this much meat."

"Maybe one of these nights you can invite me over for dinner and…"

She narrowed her eyes. "And what, Garrett?"

"You can show me how to make…let's say, chicken-fried steak. That's something I can't cook on a grill."

Her clear brown eyes grew wider. "You really want me to teach you to cook?"

"Yes. It doesn't have to be more than a couple of nights a week." Brynn pulled her lip between her teeth, appearing if as deep in thought as the seconds ticked. "Miss Hawkins? Are we on for a couple of nights a week?"

Brynn folded her arms under her breasts over a faded T-shirt stamped with I Love San Antonio and his gaze lingered there. "Okay. I'll agree to a couple of nights a week."

She extended her hand and, smiling, Garrett took it in his much larger one and pressed a kiss on her fingers. He was close, close enough to inhale the scent of roses and coconut on her hair and body. He'd kissed her hand when it was her lush mouth he'd wanted to taste.

"Deal," he breathed before releasing her hand.

"When do you want to begin?" Brynn asked as she took a step back to put some space between them.

Garrett was hard-pressed not to pump his fist in the air as if he'd just crossed the finish line after running a marathon. "It all depends on your schedule."

"I'm free tomorrow night."

He nodded. "Tomorrow it is. What time should I come?"

"What time do you normally eat?" Brynn asked.

He shrugged his shoulders. "It varies."

"Well, I usually eat before seven, so if you come around five, then we should be able to sit down to eat around six."

"That works for me," Garrett agreed. "Do you want me to bring anything?"

"Just yourself."

He pointed to the cooler. "Do you want me to help you unpack?"

Brynn shook her head, magnificent curls moving with the motion. "That's okay. I've got this. Do you want the cooler back or can I throw it away?"

"Because of sanitary reasons, we recommend a one-time only use."

"Oh! I'm forgetting my manners. Can I get you anything to eat or drink before you leave?" Brynn asked Garrett.

"No thanks. I'm good." Crosby had called and invited him to meet at Doug's.

"I guess that does it. I'll see you tomorrow around five?" she asked.

He wanted to tell Brynn that only something cataclysmic would keep him from seeing her. When they'd sat together at DJ's Deluxe, he'd thought it was the festive mood that had made it so easy for him to talk to her. But now, in her home, their carefree banter and conversation had continued. Something about Brynn allowed him to be himself. Completely.

There was no need to waste time playing games—
something he detested.

He nodded then turned and headed for the door.
"Yes. See you then."

Garrett made it back to his pickup and was unable
to stop grinning.

Did Brynn Hawkins turn him on?

Yes, she did. But he'd had enough experience to
control where he wanted their involvement to go—
and sleeping with Brynn was definitely not an option,
even though she was sexier than any woman he'd
known. He just had to make certain whatever they
would share would stay in the friend zone.

Brynn had just closed and locked the door behind
Garrett when her cell phone's ringtone indicated a call
from Corinne. She'd programmed a different ringtone
for each of her sisters, so she wouldn't have to glance
at the screen to see who was calling. She picked the
phone off the table in the entryway.

"Hello, Corinne."

"Do you know what someone just dropped off at
the house?"

"Yes. It's from Abernathy Meats."

"How do you know that?"

"Because I just got a delivery from them too."

"There's enough meat here to last us through the
winter and beyond. Now, if the entire Hawkins clan
lived in Bronco, all this meat would be gone in no
time."

Holding the phone to her ear, Brynn made her

way to the kitchen and opened the top of the Styrofoam cooler with her free hand. "Garrett told me the Abernathys wanted to thank us for giving them VIP seats to the Mistletoe Rodeo and for Mom inviting them for dinner."

"All I can say is it was very generous of them to give us this much meat. I'm going online to research recipes right away."

Brynn smiled. "I'm going to give the Abernathys a gift thanking them for us when we meet with them again on Thanksgiving."

"Are you going to make something for them?" Corinne asked.

"Probably. I believe that would go over better than something I'd buy at a store."

"Audrey said the Burrises have also invited us to Thanksgiving. And she said Mike will be home from medical school during that weekend."

Now Brynn knew why Corinne was in such good spirits. She would get to see Mike again. "Going to two Thanksgiving dinners in one day will be a little tricky. Maybe we can visit the Burrises earlier in the day and then join the Abernathys later in the afternoon."

"I'm certain that will work. I'll run the idea past Audrey and see what she says. Have you spoken to Mom?"

"No. Why?"

"She left this morning to drive to Houston to spend time with Grandma Hattie. She says she'll be there through Thanksgiving."

Brynn closed her eyes for several seconds. "I'm hoping she'll make up with Dad."

"Me, too," Corinne agreed. "I don't know what went wrong with the two of them that made Mom decide to move out. And whenever I try talking to Dad about it, he just clams up."

Brynn shook her head although Corinne couldn't see her. "I'm thinking they don't want us to take sides."

"I'd never take sides when it comes to our parents. I love them both too much for that."

"Same here, Corinne. But whatever is going on with them, I hope they can resolve it, because I don't think I could deal with it emotionally if they mention divorce."

"Bite your tongue, Brynn. You know I would have a complete meltdown if that were to happen."

Brynn wondered if Corinne was still thinking about her own on-again, off-again relationship with Mike Burris. She knew her sister was totally in love with the rodeo star studying to become a doctor, but she needed to understand that medicine had become Mike's priority. "Couples always have their difficulties, regardless of whether they're married three years or thirty-three years. I'm certain Mom and Dad will eventually work out their issues and reconcile."

"Why are you always the optimist, Brynn?"

She smiled. "Because I believe that all good things come to those who wait."

"Like you? How long has it been since you were last in a meaningful relationship?"

"We're not talking about me, Corinne," Brynn countered angrily.

"There's no need to get testy. I just asked because it looked as if you and Garrett Abernathy were really into each other Saturday night."

"We were just talking."

"And while you were, Crosby mentioned that he'd never seen Garrett talk as much as he did with you."

"That's because we were discussing things." Brynn was slightly annoyed that she had to explain to Corinne that she and a man she didn't know well had had a pleasant conversation with each other over dinner.

"I'm certain you didn't notice that Garrett couldn't take his eyes off you."

"Enough, Corinne! I'm going to hang up now."

"Not before I do. And there's no need for you to get defensive because you can't acknowledge what's in front of you. Garrett Abernathy has the hots for you."

A signal indicated that Corinne had hung up.

She'd wanted to tell her sister that she did like Garrett, that she'd felt comfortable with him. And that her sisters and Garrett's brothers were hoping for something with no possibility of happening.

What Brynn couldn't understand was why was she arguing over a man who hadn't come on to her like some men she'd known. With her life and future still unsettled, she wasn't about to lose focus and start a relationship with Garrett. She didn't mind their being friends—without benefits, because she knew intimacy always signaled a definite momentous change.

It had in the past and she didn't want a repeat. Break-ups affected her performance, and if or when she re-tired from the sport, she wanted it to be as a winner.

Brynn unpacked the cooler and managed to fit ev-erything into the large freezer drawer. Garrett had mentioned he'd wanted to learn to make chicken-fried steak, so she took out a package with several round steaks to thaw for her family recipe. Brynn had be-come the designated cook for her sisters and while Audrey, Corinne and Remi had constantly grumbled that she was too bossy, the upside was that they'd never complained about her cooking. Grandma Hat-tie had taught her well.

She'd promised Garrett cooking lessons twice a week and Brynn hoped the cowboy who'd fancied him-self a grill master would earn a passing grade where he'd learn to make his favorite dishes.

Garrett walked into Doug's, saw Crosby sitting at the bar, and took the stool next to him. "It looks like it's going to be just you and me tonight."

"Tonight, and no doubt many more nights to come," Crosby replied, gripping the handle of the beer mug before putting it to his mouth and taking a swallow.

"Don't say that as if Dean, Tyler and Wes are banned from ever going out with us. They're engaged, and right now that's their priority."

Crosby snorted. "I assume I'll be flying solo after you hook up with Brynn Hawkins."

A frown settled into Garrett's features when he

met his brother's eyes. "What the hell are you talking about?"

"You and Brynn," Crosby said as he set down the mug. "Come on now, bro. Everybody's talking about you hooking with up the beautiful lady."

"Who's 'everybody'?"

"Our brothers. Even Wes was saying you were like a deer in the headlights when you looked at her Saturday night. It was as if you were the only two at the table, ignoring everyone and everything."

Garrett wanted to use a few choice not-so-kind words to tell Crosby his interactions with Brynn were none of his or their brothers' business. He'd never offered advice to any of them about whatever women they'd been dating, and he didn't appreciate their interference in something that wasn't going to happen. Because he had no intention of *hooking up* with Brynn.

But no amount of protesting would change their concern about what they deemed the lack of his so-called love life. Not only were his brothers talking to him about Brynn, but also his mother. Garrett knew denials wouldn't temper his family's suspicions, so, in that instant, he took a different approach.

"Brynn and I are not 'hooking up,' as you put it, but she has offered to give me cooking lessons."

Crosby stared at Garrett as if he'd never seen him before and burst out laughing. "You're kidding me, aren't you?"

Garrett knew he'd shocked his brother. "I'm not kidding." He gave Crosby a truncated version of the conversation he'd had with Brynn when he'd delivered the beef. How she'd complained it was too much meat for her, and how his solution was for her to teach him to cook chicken-fried steak.

"Well, damn, Garrett. Do you realize you were about as subtle as a runaway train?"

"I only offered to help her eat the food"

"How often will you have to attend class?"

"Only twice a week. I hope—"

"What you having, handsome?" An attractive young server preempted what he was saying to Crosby.

"I'll have what my brother is drinking." He didn't recognize the woman and assumed Doug had recently hired her.

The server wiped off the top of the mahogany bar before she pulled a tap, filled a mug and set it on a coaster. "I haven't seen you around before."

"That's because his girlfriend has him on a short leash," Crosby said, grinning from ear to ear.

Garrett didn't know whether to pick Crosby up and deposit his ass on the haunted stool to scare the hell out of him, or to go along with what was a blatant lie. Smiling, he nodded and then shrugged his shoulders. It was apparent Crosby's statement had gotten through to her when she turned on her heel and walked down the bar to flirt with another customer.

His brother nudged his arm. "You could say 'Thank you, Crosby.'"

Garrett looked at him. "Why should I thank you?"

"Because I just saved you from becoming trapped in a web from which there is no escape."

"Are you speaking from experience?"

Crosby took another swallow of beer. "No comment."

Throwing back his head, Garrett laughed loudly when his brother lowered his eyes and pretended interest in the coaster. "If she flirted with you, little brother," he said in a quiet voice after he'd recovered from laughing, "then you didn't have to flirt back."

Crosby slipped off his stool. "Let's get a table and order something to eat."

Garrett followed him to a table, unable to stop smiling. Whenever he came to Doug's, he always had a fun time. Doug's was like the bar in the television series *Cheers*. It was where everyone knew everyone's name. Those new to Bronco could drive or walk right past it without noticing the place, named and operated by eightysomething Doug Moore. It had become a landmark hangout in Bronco Valley with a storied history. There was the legend of a haunted bar stool that caused tragedy to anyone who occupied it. It sat in a corner roped off by yellow caution tape and the regulars that frequented Doug were aware that those who ignored the superstition faced the possibility of divorce, death and abject poverty.

Garrett thought about when he and his brothers had come to Doug's following Charity John winning the title of Miss Bronco at the Red, White and Bronco beauty pageant held every year on the second of July at Bronco City Park. It had become a day to remember when later that night someone had thrown a rock through the window. He and some of the patrons had gone outside to see if they could find the vandal, but he or she had disappeared.

A lot had changed since that momentous night. Evy Roberts, who'd been a waitress at Doug's, was now engaged to his brother Wes. She'd subsequently given Doug her notice when she opened her dream boutique, Cimarron Rose, in Bronco Valley.

Garrett and Crosby ordered another round of beer to go with their burgers and fries. At that moment he recalled Brynn telling Tyler that she wanted to eat at the Library, and Garrett wondered if she would enjoy spending time at Doug's. She'd told his brother she wasn't as impressed by a fancy restaurant as she was with tasty food. Bronco had its share of restaurants, but Garrett loved the food and drink at Doug's bar.

Garrett drained his mug. "The next time I come, I'm going to order the chili burger you got."

The cook smashed two burgers on the flattop, grilled them until they were crispy around the edges, and then slathered them with chili that had been cooking for hours. He topped everything with diced onions and a mound of shredded Monterey Jack cheese. For that, Garrett would throw caution to the wind when it came to cholesterol.

Crosby nodded. "Whenever I come here, I try to order the chili burger. A few times they've run out of chili, so now I call ahead to ask if it's on the menu."

"So that's why you wanted me to meet you this early."

"There is a method to my madness. Put your money away," Crosby said as Garrett rose slightly to take out his money clip. "Tonight's on me." He signaled for their server and gave her enough to cover their check.

"Thanks, Crosby." He removed a bill from the clip and left it on the bar for the flirty waitress.

She scooped up the money, smiling. "Thanks, cowboy. Come back again when she loosens the leash."

Garrett took off his Stetson and swatted Crosby with it. "See what you started."

Crosby nimbly stepped away before Garrett could hit him again. "Telling her you have a girlfriend is the perfect cover for you because everyone knows you don't flirt or pick up women."

"What I don't do is date," Garrett said as they walked to their trucks.

Crosby stopped beside Garrett's Ram and gave him a rough hug. "Thanks for hanging out with me."

Garrett returned the hug. "Are you going back to the ranch?"

A sly smile lifted the corners of Crosby's mouth. "Nah. I have a stop to make before I go home."

Shaking his head, Garrett chuckled. "If you can't be good, then be careful."

"Not to worry, bro. I'm always careful."

He watched Crosby swagger across the lot and climb into his vehicle before getting into his own. Crosby reminded Garrett of Wes. They both didn't take life too seriously—that was until the love bug bit Wes hard once he met Evy. Garrett knew that time would come for Crosby, too, when he finally met a woman who would make him assess his life as a care-free bachelor.

He knew his brothers' eventual marriages had a better chance of surviving than his because they were older than he'd been and had had more life experience before taking the plunge. He'd only been, a recent college graduate and engaged to his high school sweetheart.

Garrett drove back to the ranch and discovered Max waiting for him on the porch. "Come inside, buddy. It's time for your dinner."

He fed the dog and then went upstairs to shower and change into a pair of sweats. His nighttime routine seldom varied from catching up with the local and national news before he switched to a sports channel. He heard Max barking and went downstairs to let him out. Garrett ignored the bite of chilly air as he waited on the porch for his pet to return.

His mother's concern about him spending time alone was baseless. He had Max, Tecumseh, his brothers and his parents. And then there were his future sisters-in-law, nieces and countless Abernathy cousins. What Hannah didn't realize was that, at forty-three, Garrett was comfortable living his life and he had no intention of changing it.

Max finally returned and instead of stretching out in front of the fireplace, he went into the mudroom and settled down on a large doggie pillow. Garrett left the door open that connected the mudroom to the pantry and kitchen and returned to his bedroom.

He turned off the television and picked up a back

issue of *Farm and Ranch Living* from the stack on a side table. Hutch had a subscription to the magazine going back years and Garrett made it a habit to bring some home to read. He read two issues before he turned off the lamp and got into bed. What should've been a restful night's sleep was disturbing when he dreamed about making love with Brynn Hawkins.

He sat up, groaning when he realized his body had betrayed him again. Garrett got out of bed and went to take an ice-cold shower. And once he returned to bed, it was to sleep undisturbed by the image of the woman who had begun to haunt his dreams.

Chapter Six

The faint scent of Garrett's cologne wafted to Brynn's nostrils when she opened the door and she tried to ignore the tingling in the pit of her stomach as she met his gaze, which was as soft as a caress. Whenever he'd stared at her like this, from under lowered lids, she'd felt something sensually intense in his entrancement. It wasn't only her imagination or her decision to share nothing more with Garrett than friendship that made him so intriguing to her.

"Please come in." Nothing in her voice or expression indicated she was struggling to prove to herself that she was immune to the hunky rancher. Brynn recalled Corinne's earlier remark. *I'm certain you didn't notice that Garrett couldn't take his eyes off you.* At the moment, the same could be said for her.

Garrett handed her a decorative shopping bag. "I know you said not to bring anything, but I just didn't want to come empty-handed." Shrugging off his jacket, he hung it and his Stetson next to Brynn's puffy jacket on a coat tree.

Brynn peered into the bag to find four bottles of wine. "Thank you. I have a couple of bottles chilling in the fridge just in case you want to have some with dinner. I also have beer and green tea flavored with passion fruit."

"I'd like to try the tea."

"I was hoping you'd say that." She smiled. "Now, are you ready for your first lesson?"

"Yes."

Garrett had said yes when, if he'd been listening to the common sense voice in his head, he would've said no and turned on his heel and walked out of Brynn's apartment for the last time.

It wasn't until he'd woken earlier that morning and spent time riding Tecumseh in an attempt to clear his head, that he'd realized the dream in which he was making love with Brynn had unnerved *and* frightened him. And tonight, when she'd opened the door, it was as if he were seeing her for the first time. She'd pulled her hair off her face in a ponytail, and with the hairstyle and her bare face, she appeared even younger than before. However, it was the opposite with her figure. There was no mistaking that she was a woman.

But he couldn't leave, not when he was experiencing something he'd never felt with any woman. It was as if Brynn connected with him on a level that made him feel so incredibly comfortable; she was so easy to talk to and be with.

Garrett followed Brynn inside, noticing that she'd set two place settings on the dining table. He'd only caught a glimpse of crystal candlesticks, vases and an exquisite wine decanter on the mahogany credenza before he entered the spacious modern kitchen.

Brynn handed him a black pinstriped apron. "You should put this on. I wouldn't want you to get food on your clothes."

He unfolded the bibbed apron, slipped it over his head and looped the ties around his waist. Garrett watched as she put on a matching apron, the ties circling her waist twice before she secured them.

"Before we start, I'll need for you to wash your hands. You can use the bathroom down the hall and on the right."

He hesitated. "Are you going to demonstrate while I watch?"

"No, Garrett. You will be responsible for preparing tonight's dinner." Garrett mumbled an expletive. "I heard that, Mr. Abernathy. If you want to learn to make chicken-fried steak, I'll talk you through the process step by step. And you can't have the steak without the gravy and mashed potatoes. You'll make those, too. I'll prepare a salad and make a side of garlicky green beans and cornbread."

Garrett swore again, this time in his head. He was under the impression that, as the instructor, she would show him how to make the steaks; however, that wasn't her intention. Clearly, his lesson would be hands-on.

"You're a coldhearted woman, Brynn Hawkins."

"Yeah, yeah," she drawled, smiling. "I told you I usually finish eating before seven, so it's time for you to begin your first lesson."

Garrett resisted the urge to salute her. She'd admitted her sisters thought her bossy and he was witnessing firsthand that particular personality trait. "Yes, ma'am."

He washed and dried his hands on a towel from a stack on a low table, and returned to the kitchen where Brynn stood at the island tearing lettuce leaves. Garrett held up both hands. "I'm ready, boss."

Brynn scrunched up her nose. "Very funny." She handed him a pair of disposable gloves. "You're going to need those when you're working with the steak. The first thing I'd like you to do is peel some potatoes. After they're peeled, you'll rinse and cut them into quarters."

Garrett picked up a vegetable peeler and went to work.

Brynn curbed the urge to moan aloud as she slowly chewed the tender piece of thin, fried beef covered with a creamy gravy seasoned with salt and a lot of black pepper. Garrett had followed her instructions to the letter and the chicken-fried steak and fluffy whipped mashed potatoes were lip-smacking good. She'd complimented herself on the garlicky stir-fried green beans, warm buttery cornbread, and salad with the restaurant-quality, classic creamy Caesar dressing she'd made earlier that afternoon.

She touched a napkin to her mouth. "I've forgotten how much I love chicken-fried steak."

Garrett refilled his glass with chilled green tea. "Then I'm glad I suggested it. Your side dishes aren't too shabby either," he said, smiling.

"If you like those green beans, you should try my couscous. That, and hummus and baba ghanoush are my favorite veggie dishes."

"I had couscous for the first time when I lived in New York, and I really liked it."

Brynn stalled her fork on its way to her mouth and gave him a questioning look. "You lived in New York?"

A beat passed before he said, "Yes."

"How long ago did you live there?"

Garrett's expression changed, his easy smile becoming a mask of stone. "Ten years. It was before my divorce."

Brynn stared wordlessly across the table at Garrett. With his mention of divorce, it appeared as if all of the warmth in the room had been sucked out, replaced with an icy chill that had erased what had been easygoing camaraderie. They'd just spent almost two hours together cooking, eating and drinking, and she'd never been more comfortable with a man, but now it all had come crashing down with the utterance of a single word.

"Should I assume you don't want to talk about it?" she asked Garrett.

He nodded. "You assume right."

She recalled how, at their first meeting, she'd peeked at a sadness behind his eyes and had wondered what had put it there. Now she had a feeling it had something to do with his divorce. As much as she wanted to ask him, she had to observe his right to privacy. "Then I won't pry."

Garrett nodded again. "Thank you."

Brynn forced a smile she didn't quite feel and tried to recapture the mood they'd shared before this conversation. "I must give you kudos on the steak, gravy and potatoes. Everything was delicious."

The muscles in Garrett's jaw eased when he returned her smile. "That's because I have an incredible teacher."

"Do you think you'll be able to duplicate what you made tonight for yourself?"

Garrett cocked his head at an angle. "I'm almost certain I can. But if I run into a problem making the gravy, I'll make certain to reach out for you to walk me through it."

"Making gravy is a little tricky. It took me a long time to perfect it so it's lump-free, with my grandma Hattie at my side. Once she retired from the rodeo circuit, I spent more time at her house than my own because my mother was touring with her sisters."

"Tell me about the original Hawkins Sisters. I'm curious about how you ended up following in their footsteps."

Pushing back her chair, Brynn stood. "Come with me and I'll show you."

Garrett also rose to his feet. "Where are we going?"

"You'll see."

Intrigued by what Brynn wanted to show him, Garrett followed her to a room that she'd set up as an office/workshop. A shelving unit lined an entire wall and was filled with skeins of yarn, swatches and bolts of fabric, spools of colorful ribbon, and plastic bins bursting with notions that harkened back to centuries-old general stores. There were sewing and cutting machines on a drop-leaf table and, positioned near a window, there was a weaving loom with an unfinished rug in a Southwestern diamond pattern. There was another table in a corner with a collection of quilts and throw pillows covered with a variety of fabrics.

"Is this what you do when you're not rodeo riding?"

Brynn smiled. "Yes. This is my plan B for when I retire from the rodeo."

Garrett walked over to inspect a floor frame for hand quilting. It appeared as if Brynn was close to completing a baby's blanket. "Do you sell what you make?"

"Yes. Mostly to my friends and the people they refer."

He felt her warmth when she came over to stand next to him. "What else do you make, other than quilts and rugs?"

"Candles, soaps, wreaths and dried flower arrangements. I'd love to make pottery, too, but that requires a kiln."

Garrett shook his head in amazement. This was a side of Brynn he could've never imagined. "You are an incredibly talented woman. What made you get into crafting?"

"I fell into it in high school. I took an art class with a teacher who lectured about the history of textiles. I'd found it fascinating, and when I told my parents I wanted to go to college for textile and apparel studies, they looked at me as if I'd lost my mind, because they'd expected me to join the next generation of Hawkins Sisters on the circuit. I went back and forth with my headstrong mother and grandmother until we finally compromised. They agreed to let me attend college, but in between semesters, I would travel with them."

"Did you get your degree?"

"No. I dropped out after two years, but I never regretted it because I found two women who've become my mentors."

"So, other than your friends and their referrals do any of your sales come from social media?"

"Only a few do for now. That happens when I upload a sample of something I've made for the first time."

"What about later?"

"That's when I'd like to open a small shop."

"Are you thinking about opening it in Bronco?" Garrett thought about Evy, who had recently fulfilled her dream to open Cimarron Rose.

"Probably not."

Her response reminded Garrett of her transient lifestyle. Always on the move and performing in rodeos all over the country. "So, the talk that the Hawkinses were going to settle permanently in Bronco is just a rumor?"

"No, Garrett, it's not just a rumor. Audrey bought the house we rented when I lived there with my sisters, so she's already settled. Corinne and Remi are seriously talking about buying property in Bronco. My mother and grandmother are also thinking about moving here permanently, but that's still up in the air because my parents have separated and no one knows if they're going to get back together. You'd think, after being married for more than thirty years, they would be able to work out their differences."

Garrett heard the anguish in her voice. "I'm so sorry about your folks' breakup." And he was. Even after forty-six years of marriage, Hutch and Hannah still acted like newlyweds.

"I try not to think or talk about it." She paused. "What do you think of my plan B?"

"I think it's incredible and, just looking at what you're working on, I know you'll be successful."

Brynn smiled broadly and gave him a quick hug. He knew she meant it as a gesture of thanks, but she clearly had no idea that it had taken all his self-control to keep from touching her.

She dropped her arms and stepped back. "Now, you asked about the Hawkins Sisters, so let me show you some photographs of my family." Reaching for his free hand, she led Garrett across the room to an armoire filled with shelves of black-and-white and color family photographs spanning decades and generations.

Peering closer, he smiled when recognizing a noticeably young Brynn sitting on a pony, two fat braids falling over her narrow chest. He eased his hand from hers and pointed to the photo. "How old were you when this picture was taken?"

"I'd just turned six. It was the first time I was allowed to ride a horse by myself, and back then it was the greatest thrill of my life." Brynn pointed to another photo. "That's our matriarch, Hattie Hawkins, and the one next to it is a picture of her daughters. My grandfather, Hattie's husband, died tragically in a rodeo accident shortly after they were married, and because she was on the road during all of her childbearing years, she decided to adopt.

"My mother Josie and her sister Hollie are Black. Suzie is white and Lisa is Latina. Hattie adopted them as teenagers. They learned everything about performing under her tutelage and traveled the rodeo circuit with her as the original Hawkins Sisters."

"I like that you have a mixed-race family."

Brynn nodded. "Not too many people wanted to take in teenage foster children, but that didn't matter to Hattie. My family has continued the tradition of adoption with my mother and aunties, although they have biological children of their own, too. Audrey and I are my parents' biological daughters, but they also adopted Corinne and Remi. They were one and two at the time, too young to remember their biological mother. She was a horse trainer who was killed in a tragic riding accident."

"Do you intend to continue the tradition of adoption?" Garrett questioned.

Brynn smiled. "Yes. Adoption has been such a blessing for our family. I wouldn't trade my sisters for anything. And I'd be proud to grow my family through adoption."

Garrett had promised himself that he wouldn't compare Brynn to Faith, but this time he couldn't help himself.

He cocked his head and gave Brynn a direct stare. "You're just full of surprises, aren't you, Miss Hawkins? Good ones."

She smiled. "That's because what you see is not what you get." She tilted her delicate chin and met his eyes. "That's been a problem in my life. I've been involved with some men who tried putting me in a particular box, and once they discovered that I refused to fit into their mold, all hell would break loose. That's one of the reasons I no longer date rodeo cowboys."

"Are you dating anyone now?"

Brynn shook her head. "No. Why are you asking?"

He shrugged. "Just curious."

"Curious about what?"

Garrett realized Brynn had just put him on the spot and, outspoken as she was, he knew she expected a direct answer. "Just wanting to know if there's someone who'd be upset if we became friends. Despite our age difference, that is." He paused. "I am thirteen years older than you."

Her eyebrows lifted questioningly. "Age is just a number, and I'll have to think about it."

"What is there to think about?" he questioned.

"If you're expecting benefits. And if you are, then I'm not the friend for you."

Garrett shook his head. "No benefits, Brynn." His intent was not to go down that route again with any woman, no matter how much he dreamed about them.

Brynn knew she'd lied not only to herself but also to Garrett when she said she'd wanted a platonic relationship. Everything about the man was an erotic turn-on and if circumstances had been different for her, she would've left the door open for them to be friends with the possibility of benefits, even he'd felt she was too young for him. However, the timing wasn't right. She was one of the Hawkins Sisters and she was committed to performing with them.

She'd discovered Garrett was so different from the two men with whom she'd had relationships. He was definitely more mature than her exes, who'd complained that she didn't know how to have fun. What they'd thought of fun, she'd found revolting. Binge drinking and frequenting strip clubs were not on her list for how she'd wanted her boyfriends to spend their free time.

Garrett broke into her thoughts with a question. "When do you have to leave Bronco for your next rodeo?"

"Not until December. Why?"

"Whenever you decide to take a break from your

projects, I'd like to offer my services as your Bronco tour guide."

Brynn wondered why he'd made the offer sound so formal, as if he were introducing himself to a group of tourists. "Are you going to set up an itinerary for the tour?" she teased. He smiled, and the tenderness in his expression caused her heart to pump a runaway rhythm that made her feel warm all over.

"Nah. I thought we'd take it day to day and see what happens. Do you have anything planned for this weekend?"

"No. Why?"

"Have you been to Doug's?"

Brynn nodded. "I've been there a couple of times."

"This Saturday, I'd like to take you to Doug's, and also to the Flying A on Sunday so you can meet Tecumseh and Max."

"Tecumseh and Max?"

"My horse and my dog."

"What made you name your horse after a legendary Native American chief?"

"Tecumseh happens to be an Appaloosa."

Brynn's features became even more animated. "Appaloosas are my favorite horses."

"Then you'll definitely like Tecumseh. We bred him with an Appaloosa mare on another ranch in Bozeman and earlier this year we introduced a new colt to our ranch. We named him Chief Joseph after the chief of the Nez Perce tribe. I've been trying to get the rancher to sell the dam, and we've been going back and forth negotiating a price. Last week I gave him my final offer."

"You have cattle, horses and bison on the Flying A?"

"Yup."

"That's a lot of hooves on the ground."

Throwing back his head, Garrett laughed. "Not to worry, Brynn. The Abernathys own enough grazing land."

"Well, I'm looking forward to meeting all your animals. And to seeing your ranch." After all, the Abernathys were renowned cattle ranchers, some of Big Sky Country's finest. But, if she were honest, she was most looking forward to spending the day with the rancher himself.

And that thrilled her and frightened her at the same time.

After a few minutes, as Garrett continued to study the photos of the Hawkins family, she asked, "Would you care for some dessert?"

He glanced at her over his shoulder. "We're having dessert?"

Brynn smiled. "Don't look so surprised. Of course, we're having dessert. I'm sure when you were growing up your mother made dessert for you."

Garrett stood straight. "If she didn't, then there was certain to be a family mutiny led by my father." He smiled. "Even to this day, I still don't know how she managed to remain sane after raising five rambunctious boys."

"Raising them on a ranch is a lot easier than in a house or in an apartment. And I'm sure you guys had assigned chores that kept you busy and out of trouble when you weren't in school."

"That's for certain. Mucking out stalls, mending and replacing fence posts, rigging and baling hay, and branding didn't leave much time for troublemaking."

"I'm sure you've hired ranch hands to do most of the heavy lifting now."

"Not really. The Flying A is a family ranch, and we still work the land. During the summers, we'll hire high-schoolers or college kids who are interested in animal husbandry. We do have employees, but they work at Abernathy Meats."

"Do you live on the ranch?"

"Every generation of Abernathy has lived on their ranches. Kids grow up and build homes on the land and raise their families there."

Brynn stared at Garrett in astonishment. "It's like growing up and never leaving home."

Garrett slowly shook his head. "It's more than that, Brynn. All of us have homes on the ranch, but there's enough distance between us that we'd have to walk at least a mile to see one another."

Her eyes grew wide as her jaw dropped. "The Flying A is *that* big?"

Garrett smiled. "It's large enough for everyone to be assured their privacy."

"I suppose that works whenever y'all want to bring a woman home."

Garrett sobered. "I suppose that works for some of us."

Brynn knew that she'd hit another sore spot with

Garrett. Was it because of his ex-wife? They'd decided to be friends and not lovers, so there was no need for her to know about the woman who'd once been Mrs. Garrett Abernathy.

"So, are you passing on coffee and dessert?"

"No way," he countered.

"I'm going to pack up the leftovers for you to take home."

"When is the next cooking lesson?"

"How about next Wednesday?" She needed some time to finish quilting the crib blanket she was making for a friend.

"Wednesday's fine with me. What will I be making?"

"Oxtail stew with steamed rice and smothered cabbage. Should I assume you've had oxtail before, since you'd included them in the delivery?"

Garrett nodded. "Of course. But I've never made rice."

Brynn patted his shoulder. "Not to worry, cowboy. Once you're finished with your lesson, you and Carolina Gold with become fast friends."

He chuckled. "Like us?"

"Let's take this one lesson at a time. We still have to see whether we can be friends," she added.

Garrett affected a snappy salute. "Yes, ma'am."

Forty-five minutes later, after sharing coffee and scoops of apple crisp, Brynn closed and locked the door behind Garrett. She smiled as she headed for the kitchen to put up the dishwasher. The feeling of closeness she'd felt with Garrett when they'd cooked together hadn't dissipated with his departure.

Not only was she comfortable talking with Garrett, she was comfortable around him, and Brynn was looking forward to touring Bronco with him. She hadn't spent as much time in the city as her sisters; whenever she hadn't been practicing or performing, she been at home working on her craft projects.

Garrett had mentioned taking her to Doug's over the weekend, although she'd been there before, and she suspected it was a favorite Bronco hangout for him and the other Abernathys.

She knew her sisters would tease her about hanging out with Garrett, but she didn't care. She was an emancipated adult responsible for her own physical, financial and emotional well-being. And intuition told her that Garrett would be good for her.

Chapter Seven

"You'd drive right past this place if you didn't know it was here."

Garrett reached for Brynn's hand as they walked across the street to Doug's bar. "Folks have said it's Bronco Valley's best-kept secret and, unlike DJ's Deluxe on Saturday nights, you don't need a reservation to get a table."

He'd called Brynn the day before to inform her to dress casually, that he'd planned to pick her up at six and take her to Doug's. And he was more than curious to see her reaction for himself to what some called a dive bar although she'd admitted to being there before. He gave Brynn a sidelong glance. Nighttime temperatures hovered below freezing and she was dressed for the weather, wearing all black: stretchy long-sleeved turtleneck, jeans, boots, and a faux-fur vest over a corduroy jacket. The dramatic color made her appear taller, slimmer, while her signature curls were secured in a ponytail.

"How often do you come out here?" Brynn asked as Garrett reached above her head to open the door.

"Maybe four or five times a month."

"That makes you a regular," she said over the raised voices and country music filling the bar.

It was barely six thirty and all of the stools at the bar were occupied, as well as all the tables. Garrett put his arm around Brynn's waist and steered her to the bar where they stood two deep. He was about to call out to the bartender when a familiar voice called his name. He turned to see Dean beckoning him. He was at a table with Susanna.

"Dean's here with Susanna."

Rising on tiptoe, she pressed her mouth close to Garrett's ear. "Did you know they were coming tonight?"

He shook his head. "Mind if we go sit with them?"

When Brynn had agreed to go out with Garrett, she hadn't anticipated running into any members of his family. But then, she thought, why not? It was Saturday night, and his brothers may have wanted to kick back and enjoy a night out much like those standing shoulder-to-shoulder at the bar. She smiled when she saw Garrett and Dean exchange what she'd come to think of as bro hugs. She was still smiling when Dean pulled her close.

"We meet again," he said. "And with my brother," Dean added, closer to her ear.

Brynn nodded. "It's nice seeing you, too," she replied, totally ignoring his reference to her being with Garrett.

Susanna rose, extending her arms, and Brynn took a step and embraced her. "Hello, again."

The brunette's brown eyes sparkled like the diamond on her left hand. "I didn't think I'd see you again this soon."

Brynn returned her friendly smile. "Same here."

After spending the past weekend with the Abernathys, she hadn't expected to run into them again for a while. But Bronco wasn't that big.

Susanna rested a hand on her fiancé's arm. "Dean, could you and Garrett please get something for me and Brynn from the bar?"

Dean looked at her. "Don't you want to wait for the waitress to take our order?"

His fiancée removed her hand and placed it over her throat. "I'm really thirsty and…"

"Let's go, Dean," Garrett said. "It looks as if it's going to take a while before anyone will come to our table. What would you ladies like to drink?"

"I'll have a light beer," Brynn said.

"Make that two," Susanna chimed in.

Susanna winked at Brynn as the brothers headed to the bar. "Now we can talk woman to woman."

Brynn took off the vest and draped it over the back of her chair before she sat next to Susanna, suspecting Dean's fiancée was more than curious to find out why she was at Doug's with Garrett. If her sisters were all up in her business about Garrett Abernathy, then she believed it was the same with his brothers and their significant others.

"I suppose you want to know about me and Garrett," Brynn said, deciding to take the initiative.

Susanna lowered her eyes at the same time pinpoints of color dotted her pale cheeks. "You certainly don't bite your tongue, do you?"

"I didn't mean to insult you but—"

"You didn't, Brynn," Susanna interrupted. "I just wanted to warn you that there's going to be a lot of talk—maybe I should say 'gossip'—about you dating Garrett, because everyone knows he doesn't date."

Brynn was curious why Garrett did not date. "It's not what you think. We're not dating. Garrett and I are just friends."

Susanna blinked slowly. "Really?"

Brynn curbed the impulse to laugh at Dean's fiancée's stunned expression. "Yes."

"Is that something you want?"

"It's something we both want. I'm involved with the rodeo and, depending upon my schedule, I could be away from Bronco for weeks or sometimes a month, and in my book that is not conducive for a successful relationship. Then I have other interests that consume a lot of my free time."

"If that's the case, why are you here with Garrett?"

"He's offered to take me around Bronco so I can make up my mind whether I want to live here permanently."

As she leaned back in her chair, a hint of a smile lifted the corners of Susanna's mouth. "So, Garrett appoints himself as your personal tour guide when I would've been more than willing to show you around."

"If we'd been sitting together at DJ's Deluxe and we'd had a conversation about Bronco, I could've agreed to hang out with you." Other than her sisters, Brynn hadn't connected with other women in Bronco who were close to her age.

Susanna chuckled. "But that didn't happen because you and Garrett were so into each other that all of us could've stripped naked and danced on the table and you never would've noticed."

Brynn shook her head. "You're just like my sisters."

"How's that?"

"They've been beating their gums about me and Garrett getting together, and I'm going to tell you what I told them."

"And that is?"

"That's not happening."

"Why not, Brynn? Garrett is an incredible guy. And not because he's going to be my brother-in-law once I marry Dean."

"I'm not saying he isn't, but for some other woman. I like Garrett as a friend and that's all."

Susanna stared at the diamond ring on her left hand. "It was the same with me and Dean for more years than I could count, and one day everything changed when he stopped relating to me as his younger sister and finally saw me as a grown woman."

"What happened to change everything?"

Susanna leaned closer. "I see Dean and Garrett coming back with our drinks. I work for the Bronco Theater Company, so before you leave, I'll give you my cell number and hopefully we can get together and chat," she whispered.

Brynn nodded. "Okay." She thought about what Susanna had said about Garrett not dating and wondered if it was because of his divorce or if his subsequent relationships had soured him. Well, it wasn't much different from her own experience.

Brynn knew she'd shared some of the blame for the failure of her prior relationships because there were things she deemed unforgivable, some things she refused to compromise on. She didn't believe in "out of sight, out of mind" and infidelity was a definite deal breaker. For her, there was no guarantee a cheating boyfriend wouldn't also become a cheating husband.

Her sisters had scoffed when she'd told them she was unable to love someone more than she loved herself. And that meant she had to be content with her life before she was willing to share it with someone else.

She smiled when Garrett set her beer on the table and then sat beside her. "I asked for a mug for you because I wasn't certain you'd want to drink from a bottle."

She touched the icy mug to his bottle. "Thank you, but I don't have a problem drinking from a bottle."

Garrett draped his free arm across her shoulders. "That's my girl."

Dean lifted his bottle. "To love and family."

Brynn hesitated then raised her mug. If Dean was

talking about love, then it had to be about him and Susanna. Judging how he looked at her, there was no doubt she'd captured the heart of the handsome rancher.

She considered telling Garrett to remove his arm, but didn't want to bring attention to her increasing uneasiness. She didn't mind being seen with him, but she wasn't comfortable with people seeing them hugged up as if they were a couple.

"What do you recommend I order, Garrett?" she asked.

"The chili burgers are phenomenal."

A server finally approached the table to take their orders. "So," she said, "you're the girlfriend that has your boyfriend on a short leash."

Brynn realized the woman was talking about her. "Excuse me?"

The woman smiled, leaning over the table. "I'd like to know your secret for getting your man not to look at another woman."

"We'd like you to take our orders now," Garrett said, a slight edge in his voice.

Brynn was totally confused, wondering if Garrett and the woman had had something in the past, but then recalled Susanna stating that Garrett didn't date. The tense moment ended when the server took their orders and left.

"What was that all about?" Dean asked.

Garrett ran a hand over his face. "That's some crap Crosby concocted when I met him earlier this week. When she mentioned that she hadn't seen me before, our brother told him that my girlfriend had me on a short leash."

Dean couldn't stop grinning. "It worked, didn't it? When I came here a couple of weeks ago with Wes and Tyler, I did notice that she's an incurable flirt."

"Was she flirting with you?" Susanna asked Dean.

"Nah, babe. Most folks in Bronco know that three of Hutch Abernathy's five boys are headed for the altar." He turned to Brynn. "Did you know Wes's fiancée used to work here before she opened her boutique?"

"What does she sell?" Brynn asked.

"Most of her clothes are bohemian-cowgirl-chic," Susanna said.

"Where's her shop, Susanna?"

"It's called Cimarron Rose and it's here in Bronco Valley. If you want, we can go there together."

Brynn smiled. "I'd like that. Let me know when you're available." Even though she favored jeans and boots, Brynn did have a fondness for boho tops and dyed floral-print maxi dresses.

Susanna winked conspiratorially. "Okay."

Garrett wound a curl in Brynn's ponytail around his finger. "I'd planned to take you to Evy's shop, but since you're going with Susanna, I can cross that off my list."

Turning her head, Brynn met his eyes. "I'm certain there are plenty of other places in Bronco for me to see."

He smiled. "You're right about that."

She was sure Garrett registered her sigh of relief

when he removed his arm. "What's up with the stool and the caution tape at the end of the bar?"

Susanna frowned. "I hope you all are not going to start with that superstitious nonsense about the Death Seat."

Dean nodded at his fiancée, then turned to Brynn. "I'm curious—are you familiar with the rumors about Bobby Stone?"

Brynn nodded. "Somewhat. I saw the Remember Bobby Stone flyers plastered around the Bronco Convention Center several months back and then there was talk during the Mistletoe Rodeo that folks either saw him or his ghost at the back of the arena."

"Bobby Stone was last seen drinking heavily while sitting on that stool," Dean explained. "And he was well aware of the legend that it was haunted."

"Haunted how?" Brynn asked.

"Folks who sat on it either died suddenly, got divorced, or lost all their money."

Like Susanna, Brynn didn't believe in superstitions. "What happened to Bobby Stone?"

"There were rumors that Bobby died while hiking in the mountains outside the city," Garrett said.

Brynn shook her head. "Rumors don't translate into evidence, Garrett. Unless someone can produce Bobby Stone's body, then he should be listed as a missing person."

Susanna gave Brynn a fist bump. "My sentiments exactly."

"Someone has been watching too many true crime shows," Dean said under his breath.

* * *

If it had been a weeknight, Garrett would've lingered as long as possible at Doug's to spend more time with Brynn, but he'd overheard some of the wait-staff talking about a long wait for a table. Fortunately, Brynn had agreed to go with him to the ranch the next day and then, on Wednesday, he would return to her apartment for his second cooking lesson.

Garrett drove Brynn back to her apartment then headed for the Flying A. She'd thanked him for an enjoyable evening and opened and closed the door so quickly, it was as if she'd feared he would attempt to kiss her. He didn't need the reminder that she wanted a friend, not a boyfriend.

His cell phone rang, the number appearing on the pickup's dashboard screen as he turned onto the road leading to his cabin. "What's up, Dean?"

"I like her."

"Of course you'd like Susanna if you're planning to marry her."

"I'm talking about Brynn. She's really good for you."

"Is Susanna there with you?"

"No. I dropped her off at Tyler's because she said she wanted to talk to Callie about some wedding stuff. Why?"

"Have you been talking to our mother?"

"No. Why?" Dean repeated.

"Because Mom said the same thing to me about Brynn being good for me."

"Are you denying it, Garrett?"

"I'm not going to deny that I like her."

"What are you going to do about it?"

"Nothing. Brynn and I are friends."

"With or without benefits?"

"Do you really expect me to answer that question?" Garrett was beginning to resent his family questioning him about Brynn.

"I really don't mean to pry—"

"Then don't, Dean." Garrett let out a breath. "Look, I know being seen out and about with Brynn will generate a lot of talk and…" His words trailed off.

"And everyone knows that you don't date."

"I don't date. But folks aren't going to believe that when they see me and Brynn together."

"That's exactly what I'm telling you, big brother. Just go with the flow and enjoy yourselves. I'm glad you like her and enjoy her company because there's something special about Brynn."

Garrett had to agree with Dean. Brynn was special. Special enough for him to be seen in public with her. He also knew if he hadn't been an Abernathy, people wouldn't care who he dated.

"You're right, Dean. I'll go with the flow and let people think whatever they want."

"I'm certain Mom will be glad to hear that because now she can stop complaining that you spend too much time alone."

Garrett smiled. "Our mother has too many kids to concentrate on one."

"True. But you have to remember you were her

only child for eight years before I came along. So that makes you special."

"So special that she had four more kids only a few years apart."

"That's because she and Dad were trying for a girl."

"Can you imagine it if we'd had a sister, Dean?"

"Nope. I'm certain once she was old enough to date, Dad would've put a tracking device on her vehicle to monitor her whereabouts. Have you seen him with Maeve and Lola? He adores those two little girls."

Garrett knew Dean was right. Hutch Abernathy had become a complete mush when it came to his granddaughters. "He and Mom are already talking about what they want to buy them for Christmas."

"Speaking of Christmas… It's not that far away, and I have to find something special for Susanna."

"You can never go wrong with jewelry." Garrett recalled the times Faith had left little notes around the house about what she'd wanted for Christmas or her birthday. And it was always a piece of jewelry.

"You're right about that, Garrett. I'll go back to Beaumont and Rossi's to find something nice for her."

The high-end jewelry store was where most of the wealthy ranchers purchased engagement and wedding rings, and the occasional bauble for birthdays and anniversaries. And it was where Dean had bought Susanna's diamond ring.

Garrett chatted with his brother for another minute before ending the call.

Max was waiting for him when he tapped the remote device on the pickup's visor to open the garage door. The dog ran inside and waited for Garrett on the steps leading to the mudroom.

He gave his trusted companion a gentle pat on the head. "I need you to be on your best behavior tomorrow because I'm having company." Max responded with a low bark. "You'll like her, boy, because I like her."

And Garrett did like Brynn. A lot more than he was willing to admit.

Brynn, having changed into a pair of lounge pants with a matching shirt, sat on the living room sofa watching *Tower Heist* on the flat-screen atop the mahogany console with its electric fireplace. It was a film she'd seen before and there were enough comedic scenes to make her laugh so she wouldn't have to dwell on her outing with Garrett. She'd thought of it as an outing rather than a date because, after all, friends did spend time together.

She knew agreeing to and maintaining a friendship with Garrett wasn't going to be an easy feat. It would take determination and an iron will not to allow her growing attraction to overwhelm her senses. His masculine good looks aside, Brynn was drawn to his subdued confidence. He was more than comfortable with his family's wealth and status in Bronco—and felt no need to show it off. Garrett and Dean appeared as contented drinking beer from a bottle at Doug's as they had sipping wine from a fragile wineglasses at DJ's Deluxe.

Brynn was intrigued by Susanna's revelation that Garrett didn't date. He didn't date, yet he didn't seem bothered about going out with a woman. She wondered if he was sending her a double message. He wanted her as a friend, not a girlfriend. But when she'd decided she'd wanted friendship, it was without benefits because she knew sleeping with Garrett would dredge up some of her insecurities that she was unlucky when it came to love.

Once her last relationship had ended, Brynn had poured out her heart to her grandmother. Hattie had reminded her that she had to learn to love with her head as well as her heart, and all that was good to her wasn't necessarily good for her. It had taken her a while to decipher what the older woman meant.

Sleeping with Miles Parker had been satisfying for Brynn, but what they'd shared in bed had not extended to their connection outside the bedroom. He'd treated her like a rodeo colleague and not his partner or lover. He'd claimed his manager had wanted to keep their affair private because he was growing his celebrity image while negotiating for company endorsements.

Brynn had gone along with it at first. Until the news came out that Miles had been sleeping with a number of women and had paid hush money to several who'd had his babies. That had been the proverbial straw that had broken the camel's back for her. Miles had been guilty of the trifecta of lying, cheating and secretly fathering a number of children.

She was thankful Garrett had insisted they would be friends. Friends without the pressure of them sleeping together. And if she'd continued to tell herself that being friends was something she needed, maybe she'd convince her heart that it was what she wanted.

Chapter Eight

Brynn felt as if she had been traveling for miles once Garrett passed the marker identifying the Flying A Ranch. She stared at the unfolding landscape. "Do the Abernathys own all this land?"

Garrett gave her a quick glance between returning his attention to the road. "Yes. There's the Flying A and the Ambling A."

"What the difference?"

"Both ranches are owned by Abernathys, but the Ambling A is larger, and their main house resembles what folks would call a mansion."

"And the main house at the Flying A?"

"It's a lot more modest, and it's coming up in a quarter mile on your right."

Brynn stared out the windshield at a structure that

did not come close to what Garrett had described. "How many square feet does 'modest' translate into?"

"Give or take, about six thousand."

"It's lovely." She'd said "lovely," but the Flying A's main house was nothing short of grand.

When the Abernathys had invited her family to celebrate Thanksgiving with them, Brynn had thought about making a wreath for the front door, but after seeing the expansive ranch-style home with its enormous double doors, she realized she would have to make two.

Garrett slowed the pickup and stopped near the front of house. Smiling, he winked at her. "Don't run away. I'll be right back."

If she were to run, it would take her days, if not weeks, to explore thousands of acres of forests, grazing land and mountains ranges.

Garrett returned from the side of the house carrying a large, covered wicker hamper. Wearing jeans, a blue-and-white-plaid flannel shirt, and his favored blue corduroy jacket, he appeared impervious to the chilly weather. The overcast skies hinted of either sleet or snow and Brynn had made certain to dress in layers. He opened the rear door to the heavy-duty pickup and set the hamper on the second row of seats.

"That's our picnic lunch," he said as he got in behind the wheel again.

Brynn closed her eyes, not believing what she'd just heard. The temperatures were hovering at freezing and Garrett was talking about a picnic lunch.

"Picnic, Garrett? Do you have any idea that this isn't the time of year for picnicking?"

Garrett squeezed her jeans-clad knee before shifting into gear. "Not to worry, beautiful. I'll make certain you stay warm."

Brynn did not visibly react to Garrett calling her beautiful because it was the same thing he'd said about Maeve. He'd said his niece was precious and beautiful. Brynn wasn't vain and, despite attracting a lot of male attention, had learned not to let it turn her head. Especially since she'd chosen a career in a male-dominated sport where some men were bold enough to ask her outright if she would sleep with them.

"You don't believe me, do you?" Garrett asked when she shared a glance with him.

"No comment."

"I want you to always feel safe whenever you're with me, Brynn."

She nodded. He meant he would protect her, but who was going to protect her from him if she found herself in too deep? Since being introduced to Garrett days before the Mistletoe Rodeo, she realized they were spending a lot of time together. And with each encounter, she'd discovered she really liked him more than she should, which led her to wonder if a man and woman could actually remain friends—and for how long.

"What made you decide that picnicking in Montana in the dead of winter was a clever idea?"

"My mother. And it's not winter."

"Your mother?"

"Yes Hannah Abernathy. When I told her I was going to take you on the tour of the ranch before we went riding, she recommended I bring a picnic lunch."

Brynn swallowed a moan. There was no doubt that every Abernathy now knew about her and Garrett. "What else did you tell her about us?"

"I told her you volunteered to teach me to cook and, for my first lesson, I learned to make chicken-fried steak. She looked a little sad when I told her I wouldn't come around as often once I'd mastered a few dishes I really like."

"And what else did you tell her, Garrett?"

"Oh, and that I'd offered to show you around Bronco."

Brynn didn't know why that sounded like an after-thought. She was still pondering what else he'd said to his mother when Garrett came to a stop and parked near an outcropping of trees overlooking a lake.

"Please stay in the truck where it's warm until I set up everything."

Brynn unbuckled her seat belt and turned to see Garrett remove items from the pickup's cargo box. He then spread out a blanket on the ground, along with a portable propane outdoor heater. She couldn't help smiling. So, she thought, there was a method to his madness for having a picnic in freezing temperatures. He set the hamper on the blanket and then returned to the truck and turned off the engine.

Garrett opened the passenger-side door, extended his hand to Brynn, and helped her down. He looked at her for a moment, their gazes locking, before he lowered his eyes to stare at her mouth. Everything about the woman standing close enough that he could feel her moist breath against his bared throat made him question what he was doing. He'd brought Brynn to a section of the ranch where few ventured because he'd wanted some alone time with her. He thought of her as an onion where he would have to peel off each layer one at a time to discover who she actually was. She'd warned him that what he saw wasn't necessarily what he would get.

"Are you ready to eat?"

Brynn's lips parted as she smiled. "Yes. And I apologize."

His eyebrows rose questioningly. "For what?"

"For doubting you, Garrett, when you said you'd make certain I stayed warm."

"Even though it's not necessary, I accept your apology." He led her over to the blanket, holding on to her arm as she sat.

"It's amazing that this stove gives off so much heat."

Garrett sat beside Brynn and removed his hat and jacket. "I use it and several others whenever I grill outside during the winter."

Brynn gave him an incredulous look. "You grill in the winter?"

"Weather permitting, I grill year-round. The exception is sleet and snow."

"What about rain?"

Brynn took off her Stetson, set it behind her on the blanket, and then shook out her hair. Garrett watched, transfixed by the sensual motion as a cloud of mahogany brown curls floated down her back. "I have patio umbrellas."

She smiled. "It appears as if you think of everything."

"It's called preparedness."

Stretching out her legs, Brynn crossed her booted feet at the ankles. "Do you have a kitchen in your home?"

"Of course. It's just that I prefer grilling to turning on an oven. I like spending as much time as possible outdoors." He unlatched the top of the picnic hamper and handed her a plate and a napkin. "Do you ski?"

"I have a few times."

"Do you have ski clothes?" he asked her.

"Yes. Why?"

"Once we have enough of a snowfall, I'd like to take you snowmobiling."

Brynn gave him a sidelong glance. "I've never been on a snowmobile. It sounds like fun."

"It is for me because I'm partial to winter sports." In fact, no matter the season, he felt more alive with the earth under his feet, the sky above his head.

Garrett cocked his head. "So, you approve of our chilly weather picnic?"

She smiled. "I approve and look forward to a repeat. That is…if you plan to invite me again."

"Why would I not invite you, Brynn?"

Shifting slightly, she gave him a direct stare. "I've learned not to make assumptions."

"Should I assume that comes from past experience?"

* * *

"Yes," Brynn admitted as she watched Garrett remove containers labeled as chicken, potato, and egg salad, stone wheat crackers, sliced carrots and cubed cheese from the hamper.

"What happened?" he questioned. "Or you don't want to talk about it?"

Brynn realized if she and Garrett were going to be friends, there was no reason for her not to be open with him.

"I don't mind talking about it. I was in college when a boy in my English Literature class asked if we could be study partners. He was on a scholarship and needed to maintain a B average, but he was failing Lit. I'd shared a dorm room with another girl, while he had an off-campus apartment, so we'd alternated studying in my room one Saturday afternoon and his apartment the following week. When it came time for my Saturday and he didn't show up or return any of my phone calls, I decided to go to his apartment." She paused, biting her lip to keep from laughing as she selected small portions of salad from each container.

"Was he okay, Brynn?"

"He was more than okay. He'd come to the door in his boxers and, standing behind him, butt-naked, was my roommate. I'll never forget the look on her face when she saw me. A couple of days later, she moved in with another student."

"You didn't know she'd been sleeping with your study partner?"

Brynn shook her head. "No. She'd go to the library whenever he came over to give us what she'd said was privacy. I guess she was jealous because he and I were spending time together."

"What did he say to you when you discovered them together?"

"Believe it or not, he went off on me, claiming I had invaded his privacy showing up without calling. That's when I told him if he'd checked his phone and saw that I'd left several voice mails, I wouldn't have come over. And then I told him I couldn't care less who he slept with, and he should grow up and act like a man. That's when he slammed the door in my face."

"Damn! Both of them were being deceptive."

She nodded. "Deceptive or not, the entire situation taught me not to assume anything."

"Did he pass the course?"

Brynn shook her head. "I'm sorry to say, he didn't. I don't know if he'd lost his scholarship, but I never saw him again after that semester."

"What I don't understand is why didn't he tell you he was sleeping with your roommate?"

"Probably because he was sleeping with more than one woman and if they'd found out that he was cheating on them, the situation could have become a little sticky."

"Sticky is putting it mildly," Garrett said. "I'd say it could've been dangerous. I've witnessed firsthand the fallout from cheating."

"Are you speaking from experience?" she asked.

"No. Fortunately, that's something I've never had to deal with."

"Good for you."

"What about you, Brynn?"

"What about me, Garrett?" She'd answered his question with one of her own.

"Has a man ever cheated on you?"

"Yes."

Garrett rested a hand on her back. "I can't imagine a man cheating on you."

She gave him a long, penetrating stare. "And why not? What makes me so different from millions of other women around the world when either their husbands or significant others cheat on them?"

Garrett knew he'd backed himself in a corner with the comment and now Brynn expected an answer. And just not an answer, but one that was honest. "Because you're everything a man could ever want in a woman. You're beautiful, intelligent, talented, independent, and, above all, honest. You say exactly what you're thinking, so there's no mistaking a double meaning."

"Thank you for the glowing compliment, but maybe that's not enough for some men."

"What more could they want, Brynn?"

A hint of a smile flittered across her lips. "Some men like bad girls the same way good girls like bad boys. Not only are they exciting, but they are also unpredictable."

"Are you saying you like bad boys because they're exciting?"

"I'm saying just the complete opposite, Garrett. I get enough excitement as a rodeo rider. If I were to have a boyfriend or husband, I don't want to compete with him. I know that every day isn't going to be like a fairy tale or have a rom-com ending, but it should come enough close to where I would be willing to talk through our problems and eventually compromise to make the relationship work."

"You sound very idealistic."

"That's because I'm an optimist."

"And you're probably a romantic."

"That, too," she said, agreeing with him.

Garrett wanted to tell Brynn that he, too, was once idealistic. That when married, he'd believed in happily-ever-after. But he couldn't get his mouth to form the words.

They sat silently, eating, until Brynn spoke. "Please let your mother know the salads are delicious. Especially the egg. It reminds me of the one I used to order from a deli in Greenwich Village."

"When were you there last?" he asked.

"A couple of years ago. You said you'd lived in New York. Did you like it?"

He shook his head and a beat passed as he chose his words carefully. "It wasn't so much as not liking it as it was my inability to comfortably adjust. I'd found it too crowded and much too noisy for this country boy."

"Is there anything you liked about it?"

He smiled. "The food."

Brynn laughed. "I know you're talking about pizza and hot dogs."

"Hell yeah! And don't forget the bagels."

Moaning, she closed her eyes. "The bagels are the best in the entire world."

"That's saying a lot about bagels."

"You know it's true, Garrett. I've traveled a lot with the rodeo and nobody's bagels can compare to the ones in New York. And it's the same with Chinese takeout."

"It sounds as if you really like the big cities."

Brynn met his eyes. "Not all big cities. But I do have my favorites, and New York City definitely makes the list. I also happen to like San Antonio, San Francisco, Boston, Washington, DC, and Denver."

"What about Bronco?"

"It's growing on me," she admitted. "If I decided to settle here permanently, I'd look for property with a barn for a couple of horses and an outbuilding I can use as a workshop."

"I'm certain you'd be able to find what you want either here in the Heights or the Valley."

Brynn scrunched up her nose. "The price for property in Bronco Heights might not leave me enough money to own horses."

"Did you grow up with horses?"

"Yes. My grandmother was raised on a farm in Houston and her family always had horses. I know if she moved here, she would transport some of them."

"If she does move here, then you could ask her for a couple of horses."

"Surely you jest, Garrett Abernathy. Hattie Hawkins would rather go through dental surgery without anesthesia than give up one of her horses."

His eyebrows lifted. "It's like that?"

"Yup."

"That's serious."

"Isn't it the same with the Abernathys and their cattle?" Brynn questioned.

"You're right about that. Cattle ranching is in our blood."

"And what if you weren't a rancher, Garrett? What else would you do?"

"I would be sitting behind a desk in an office, watching other people's investments."

Garrett knew he'd shocked Brynn when her mouth opened but nothing came out. He'd also shocked himself, because talking about what he'd done in New York was something he'd refused to discuss with his family. None of them knew that not only had he been unhappy but also miserable. Anytime he'd spoken to his mother, he'd given his finest acting performance and said all was good and that he was living the dream. It had been Faith who was living her dream.

"Is that what you did in New York?" Brynn questioned.

Garrett opened a bottle of chilled water. "Yes. I have a degree in finance."

"I'm not the only one full of surprises," she said, smiling.

Brynn was reminding him of what he'd said to her the night he'd come to her apartment, when she'd surprised him with what she called her plan B.

"Why would you say that?"

"Because I can't imagine you sitting behind a desk

in some corporate office not wearing your corduroy jacket."

Garrett was momentarily speechless that Brynn had figured him out. "You must be clairvoyant because that's what I disliked most about working in New York. The company had a dress code, and it was required that I wear a suit and tie that felt like a noose every time I put it on."

"I'd noticed you wore a banded-collared shirt the night at DJ's Deluxe."

A hint of a grin tilted the corners of his mouth. "And I noticed that you were quite turned out that night."

A rush of color suffused Brynn's complexion and Garrett wondered if his comment about her appearance had put it there.

Brynn stared at her plate, chiding herself for blushing—something she rarely did. And she didn't know why Garrett's compliment had affected her when she hadn't reacted to him telling her she was beautiful, intelligent and talented.

"I don't get the opportunity to wear skirts or dresses too often."

"It wasn't only the skirt, Brynn. It was also your hair and makeup. It took me a while to figure out it was you."

Brynn's body stiffened in shock. "Are you saying I usually look so busted that you couldn't imagine me—"

Garrett cut her off. "That's not what I'm saying. You have to know that you're a beautiful woman inside and out. I've met a lot of beautiful women, but there's no way they could begin to compete with you even if they were dressed in haute couture and you in jeans."

She stared at him, stunned by his bluntness, and wondered if he were sending her double messages. They were friends, yet Brynn felt as if he were surreptitiously seducing her. He may have thought his compliments were innocent, but she'd never had a man talk to her like Garrett Abernathy. He didn't hold back, saying exactly what came to mind, and that made them even more alike. She'd been accused of being bossy and occasionally brash while she'd thought of herself as unapologetically straightforward.

"Thank you for the compliment. Do you know that you're good for a woman's ego?"

"It's not a compliment, Brynn. It's a fact, and I never say things to boost a woman's ego."

Hold up, cowboy. There's no need to be so touchy. It was obvious she'd struck a nerve with him. "Point taken, Garrett."

They finished their picnic lunch in silence and Brynn felt a chill that had nothing to with the weather now that pinpoints of sunlight had pierced the low-hanging clouds to make it increasingly warmer. She didn't want to fight or debate with Garrett about things that threatened their easygoing friendship.

"Please thank your mother for a wonderful lunch," she said to Garrett as he turned off the portable heater and repacked the hamper.

"I will." He met her eyes. "Now, are you ready to see some bison before I introduce you to Tecumseh?"

Her smile was dazzling. "Yes!"

Garrett felt as if he'd been holding his breath and was finally able to exhale when Brynn smiled. He didn't know what had made him come at her like a rattler issuing a warning before it struck, and he didn't know why she tended to play down her natural beauty when some women paid thousands to achieve such perfection.

He hadn't lied when he'd said she was also beautiful inside. He knew her mother and sisters adored her and he'd noticed how quickly she and Susanna had bonded at Doug's. Whenever someone had passed their table and recognized her, she'd acknowledged them with a nod or smile.

So why couldn't he tell her he liked her? It wasn't only her age, but also her career that wouldn't allow him to open up. Her constant traveling was a reminder of how often Faith would take off for long weekends with her friends to have some fun, as if there wasn't enough fun to be had at home. So he said nothing and started up the truck.

Chapter Nine

Brynn stared at the herd of bison off in the distance, looking mesmerized. Some sat on the ground while others grazed nearby. Several calves were nursing from their mothers.

Garrett had driven her past herds of cattle and past the two-story office of Abernathy Meats. He'd showed her firsthand that the Flying A was a working ranch. She was filled with questions, her curiosity and amazement coming through with each one.

"I notice that you fence them in," she said.

Garrett nodded. "We don't want them wandering where we have the cattle. There's enough grazing acreage here for them. Bison are not domesticated animals and require different handling than cattle and other livestock. They're much more nervous and excitable in close quarters, so we need them to remain calm."

"They seem so peaceful."

"They're not extremely aggressive, though that can't be said for every herd. We take turns filling the water trough, so they've gotten used to us being around them. We also give them something known as range cake, which is like a treat. They've gotten to know us whenever we bring them goodies."

"Don't tell me that you're spoiling your bison?"

He laughed at Brynn's stunned expression. "Just allowing them to get to know us. And if we have to move them to another location, then we lure them with the range cakes, and they follow."

Brynn shook her head. "That's amazing."

Garrett wanted to tell Brynn she was amazing. She'd questioned him when he'd told her they were going to have a picnic lunch outdoors, yet she'd trusted him enough to join him.

That was what he wanted—for Brynn to trust him enough for them to enjoy a camaraderie with the freedom to live their lives. Garrett knew she would leave Bronco for the next rodeo while he remained at the Flying A, and he hoped that whenever she returned to Bronco they would be able to pick up where they'd left off.

He was still attempting to wrap his head around some man cheating on Brynn, when she was everything a normal man could want. Yes, she was sassy, but that's what made her exciting. But along with the sassiness was confidence and independence.

She knew who she was and went after whatever she wanted. On the ride over to the bison, when she'd talked about buying a house with an outbuilding she would use as a workshop for her crafts, he'd immediately thought of his cabin where there was more than enough land for him to build a workshop. Just as quickly, he'd dismissed the notion as delusion.

And at that moment Garrett knew he had to mentally get it together or he would find himself becoming emotionally involved with Brynn Hawkins, because there were too many strikes against them having a relationship. She was too young for him, she was transient, and she didn't want a sexual liaison.

He dropped an arm over her shoulders. "I think it's time I introduce you to Tecumseh and Maximus Decimus Meridius Abernathy."

Brynn's laughter echoed inside the pickup. "You named your dog after Russell Crowe's character in *Gladiator*?"

"So you're familiar with the movie?"

She gave him you've-got-to-be-kidding look. "Who isn't familiar with the movie, Garrett? I've seen it at least three times."

"I thought you were addicted to movies with romantic themes."

Brynn lifted his arm off her shoulders. "I told you before what you see isn't necessarily what you get, Garrett. Remember what happened to my boyfriend who tried to put me into a box?"

"But I'm not your boyfriend, Brynn."

No, Garrett wasn't her boyfriend. So why, in that

instant, was it exactly what he wanted to be? He'd had a strange connection with her that he'd never experienced with any other woman. He'd wanted to be able to call her up and ask her out on a date. He also wanted to forget the thirteen-year age difference. Garrett was almost certain he could become used to her traveling if she decided to make Bronco her home. Brynn had no idea that he was willing to make a number of concessions, but only if she'd agreed that she wanted more than friendship.

"You're right, Garrett. You are not my boyfriend," Brynn said.

What she didn't say to him was that she was sorry he wasn't because, if she had written criteria of what she wanted in a man, he would be able to check off every category. Brynn the Realist knew the more time she spent with Garrett, the more time she wanted to spend with him.

She glanced at his profile and saw tension had turned his expression into a mask of stone. Brynn rested her left hand over his right, which was holding the wheel in a deathlike grip. "I apologize for lumping you in that category."

Garrett reversed their hands, raised hers to his mouth and kissed the back of it. "Apology accepted."

Brynn wanted to remind him that it was the second time he'd kissed her hand. And it wasn't her hand she wanted him to kiss, but her mouth. Their eyes met and they shared a smile. But just as quickly, he released her hand and she buckled her seat belt as he shifted into Reverse and maneuvered onto a paved road.

She'd thought of the Flying A as a small town. It had paved roads, along with miles of land that reminded her of untamed wilderness before she spotted an occasional house off in the distance. She recalled Garrett's statement that the ranch was large enough for everyone to be assured their privacy, and Brynn wondered which of the homes they'd passed belonged to him.

He stopped near a barn and Brynn saw a dog she recognized as a chocolate-and-white border collie race over to the truck. She unbuckled her belt and was out of the pickup before Garrett could come around to assist her down. Going to her knees, she held out her arms. She wasn't disappointed when the dog rested his muzzle against her chest.

"You are so adorable," she crooned.

Garrett did want to believe what he was witnessing. Max was usually standoffish when it came to strangers, yet he'd taken to Brynn as if they were besties. "That's enough spoiling my dog."

Brynn glanced up at him over her shoulder. "Can you please give me and Max a moment?" Smiling, she buried her face against his neck. "Where did you get him?"

"I adopted him from a local animal sanctuary."

"Was he one of a large litter?" Brynn asked.

Garrett knelt next to Brynn and gave her sidelong glance. "Are you thinking of adopting a dog?"

She shook her head. "No. I'd never have a dog as

long as I live in an apartment. They need to be outside to run and release some energy."

"Max was only a puppy when he was found wandering through some trash in the back of a store. Someone brought him to the Happy Hearts Animal Sanctuary. When he was up for adoption, I decided to bring him home. I saw how great the pups that Wes and Susanna had adopted were and I knew I wanted one."

"What kind of dogs do they have?"

"They're Australian shepherd mix. Maggie, their mother, was a runaway and she'd managed to evade capture until she took shelter in the Bronco theater to give birth to eight puppies. Dean and Susanna were at the theater at the time, waiting out a snowstorm, and were there to witness Maggie birth her puppies."

"Both breeds are good herding dogs."

Garrett stood and nodded. Reaching down, he cupped Brynn's elbow, helping her to stand. "Max would rather cuddle or lie front of a fire than herd cattle."

"That's because this beautiful boy is spoiled," Brynn said as she patted the top of the dog's head. Amused, she said, "I hear a horse."

"Horses," Garrett said, leading her to the barn. "After the forecast of sleet this morning, we decided to stable them. I'll let them out later after I take you home."

He watched as Brynn gently stroked the neck of each horse in their stall. She stopped at Tecumseh's and smiled. "Aren't you the handsome one?"

Garrett moved closer to Brynn. "The next time you come, we can go riding."

She nodded. "Then I'll be certain to bring my saddle."

"You don't have to do that. We have dozens of saddles in the tack room to choose from."

"That's all right. I'd rather use my own."

Her insistence that she bring her own saddle was a blatant reminder to Garrett that Brynn was a rodeo rider, and a personal saddle was as important to her as a glove was for a first baseman.

"Is there anything else you'd like to see?"

Brynn shook her head. "Not today. And I really appreciate you taking the time to show me around the Flying A."

Garrett nodded. Even though they'd spent hours together, to him, it felt like mere minutes.

He drove Brynn home and she insisted he not walk her to her apartment. He sat in the truck, watching until she disappeared from his line of sight.

During the drive back to the ranch, Garrett's mind and emotions were in tumult. It was as if there were two little imaginary specters standing on each shoulder and whispering in his ears what he should and should not do.

Walk away and forget she ever existed.

Don't be a fool. Tell the woman you like her and that you want more than friendship.

In as much as Garrett wanted to call Brynn to tell her he didn't want or need cooking lessons, he realized not only would he be lying to her but also to himself.

He did want to learn to prepare meals that didn't include grilling. And he also enjoyed talking and being with her. It had been much too long since he'd been able to open up around a woman and just be himself.

She not only got him to smile more often, she was also able to make him laugh. And Brynn was challenging. She unknowingly tested him in ways he'd never permitted another woman since his divorce. This was all new for Garrett. He'd always been the one to establish what he wanted and for what duration. But with Brynn that wasn't the case. Her schedule would dictate when she was available.

He told himself it was good that there were obstacles that did not permit them to become more than platonic friends. And as long as he continued to tell himself that, he would continue to see her.

Once he reached the ranch, Garrett cradled the picnic hamper to his chest and entered the main house through the back door. He rested it on the bench and sat to remove his boots before making his way into the kitchen. His mother was standing at the island, dicing peppers.

He set the hamper on a stool before he dipped his head and kissed her cheek. "Thanks again for the picnic lunch."

Hannah smiled. "Did Brynn enjoy it?"

"We both enjoyed it." Garrett took out the empty containers, rinsed and stacked them in the dishwasher. "Brynn raved about your egg salad."

"It's probably because of the fresh dill and dill

pickle relish." She met his eyes. "When are you going to see her again?"

Garrett sat on a stool at the island. "Wednesday."

Hannah nodded. "Good."

His eyebrows rose slightly. "Good?"

"Yes," Hannah confirmed. "I know you're tired of hearing it, Garrett, but that young woman is good for you."

"That she is."

Hannah's hands stilled and she looked up at him. "You're agreeing with me?"

"I'm agreeing that she is young, Mom."

Her free hand came down hard on the granite countertop. "Stop the nonsense, Garrett! You're acting as if Brynn is some teenage girl that's jailbait. She happens to be a grown-ass woman who doesn't need you for anything because she can have any man she wants. Yet she's spending time with you. And maybe because she doesn't need you is the reason why you're acting like a fool."

Garrett stared wordlessly at his mother. It wasn't often that he saw her angry or ready to cry, but this time she appeared close to both. "I like Brynn, Mom." His voice was soft and soothing.

Hannah set the knife on the cutting board. "I know you like her, and anyone can see that she also likes you. What my sons fail to realize is that I know them better than they know themselves. I knew Dean was in love with Susanna for years and look how long it took him to realize it.

"Now, it's different with you, Garrett. Whether

you know it or not, you want a woman to need you. Faith needed you to give her a lifestyle she'd always craved. She'd believed as Mrs. Garrett Abernathy she should attend luncheons at The Association with the other rancher's wives, and chair fundraisers. The few times I'd asked her to fill in for the receptionist at Abernathy Meats, she reacted as if I'd asked her to muck out the stalls. She was so brusque on the telephone that your father called in a temp."

Garrett closed his eyes as he struggled not to lose his temper. He'd had no idea that Faith's off-putting behavior toward the customers of Abernathy Meats could have ruined their business reputation.

"Why didn't you say something, Mom?"

"This is the second time you've said that, and would you have believed me, Garrett? You only saw one side of your manipulative wife, but she knew she couldn't fool me. And I'd promised myself never to interfere in my sons' personal lives. I'd known Dean was in love with Susanna and she was in love with him, but neither of them was going to hear it from me."

Garrett knew his mother was right. "I suppose you do see things we knuckleheads can't see."

"It's not that you can't see it, it's that you don't want to see it, Garrett. It's right in front of you, but you continue to make excuses because you're afraid of making the same mistake with Brynn that you made with Faith."

"Brynn is not Faith."

"I'm glad you can acknowledge that."

Garrett knew the two women were different but for

one exception: both liked big cities. Brynn had admitted she liked New York City, San Francisco and Boston. What if she decided to move to one of those cities and she wanted him to go with her? He'd once left the Flying A because of the love for a woman, and he'd vowed never to do it again.

"What are you going to do about it, Garrett?"

He gave his mother a direct stare. "Brynn and I will continue to see each other." What Garrett didn't tell his mother was that he would continue to see Brynn as long as she lived in Bronco, and he couldn't promise anything beyond that.

Hannah smiled. "That's a good beginning."

"By the way, where's Dad?"

"He's in bed, resting his back."

Garrett's eyebrows slanted in a frown. "What happened?"

"He tried lifting a bale of hay and felt something pop," Hannah told him as she leaned over the island.

"What the hell was he doing lifting two-hundred-pound bales of hay when he has five sons?"

Hannah waved a dismissive hand. "Please don't get me started, Garrett, because you'll hear words from me that I know will shock you. He went to the doctor, who gave him some muscle relaxers that he claims make him loopy. I think he's learned his lesson now that he's flat on his back."

"I hope you reminded him that at his age he can't do the things he used to do."

Hannah made that sucking sound with her tongue

and teeth. "I will not repeat the things I told him when he came to me bent over like a pretzel."

Garrett shook his head and pushed off the stool. "I'll come by tomorrow to see how he's feeling."

"I need you to insist that he not come into the office until he's feeling better. You know he'll listen to you when he'll just ignore his other sons."

"That's because we spend more time together at the office."

"That's why I want you to fill in for him."

Rounding the island, Garrett kissed his mother's cheek. "Will do. Love you, Mom."

She smiled. "I love you, too."

Garrett put on his boots and drove back to his cabin.

He felt as if a weight had been lifted when he'd finally admitted to his mother that he liked Brynn; liked her enough to continue to spend more time with her.

Brynn hummed along with the songs on her smartphone playlist as she meticulously handstitched the baby quilt. Normally she would've resented giving up time for her crafting projects, but the hours she'd spent with Garrett were not only enjoyable but enlightening. The taciturn rancher had revealed another side of his personality she'd found irresistible. He had a way of looking at her that told her he was giving her his undivided attention. That he was truly hearing and listening to what she had to say.

Garrett had mentioned that he was thirteen years older as if it would become a barrier to their becoming friends, while to her age was always a number. And she'd lost count of the oh-so-many times she'd been referred to as an old soul. The sobriquet had bothered her as a child because she'd believed it was something bad, but as she'd gown older she'd proudly accepted the label to mean she was wise beyond her years.

Her cell phone rang and she glanced over at the screen. It was Susanna Henry. Brynn put aside the needle and thread and picked up the phone.

"Hello, Susanna."

"Did I catch you at a wrong time?"

"No. I was just relaxing. What's up?"

"How would you like to go with me tomorrow to Evy's boutique?"

"Sure. What time and where should I meet you?"

"I'll come and pick you up, say, around noon. We'll shop and then have a late lunch."

Brynn paused. "Aren't you working at the theater tomorrow?"

"Yes, but my hours are flexible."

"If that's the case, then I'll treat you to lunch at my place." Brynn figured if Susanna was going to tell her about Garrett not dating, then she would've preferred they not discuss it in a restaurant where there was the possibility of someone eavesdropping on their conversation.

"Nice move, Brynn. Eating at your place means we can talk about anyone and everything."

She smiled even though Susanna couldn't see her. "I'm glad you caught my drift."

Susanna's laugh came through the earpiece. "I'll text you once I'm close to your building."

"Okay. I'll see you tomorrow."

Brynn ended the call and then went back to quilting. As she stitched, she recalled an earlier conversation with Susanna. When Susanna had mentioned Garrett didn't date, it had made Brynn wonder why. If he'd believed their being seen together in public wasn't dating, then what was it? Whenever she was seen with the same man more than a few times, most people thought of them as dating. However, it hadn't happened with Miles because they'd managed to conceal their relationship from everyone. He'd made her promise to wait until he'd achieved the celebrity status he'd been relentlessly chasing before going public.

But his good-guy marketable image imploded once one of his baby mamas spoke up. He'd come crawling back and, in an effort to repair his image, he'd proposed marriage. Brynn had sent him on his way.

It had taken almost two years for Brynn to allow herself to be seen with a man and, unlike what she'd shared with Miles, she knew exactly where she stood with Garrett.

They were friends.

Chapter Ten

The pretty young woman with long black hair and green eyes who owned the boutique greeted Brynn with a hug when she'd walked in. "Welcome to Cimarron Rose, Brynn."

"Thank you." Brynn returned the hug then took off her jacket. Her eyes grew wide as she spotted racks of garments that were similar in style to what hung in her own closet. She turned and smiled at Evy Roberts. "I'm about to melt the numbers on all of my credit cards because I want to buy everything in your charming shop."

Evy blushed. "I hope you'll be able find something you like. And don't worry, because I'm giving you the family discount."

Brynn's jaw dropped. "That's not necessary, Evy."

Just because she'd come in with Susanna did not make her family.

"If you're dating my future brother-in-law, then you're family."

She opened and closed her mouth before telling Evy that she wasn't dating Garrett. Now, even the mention of the word grated on her. She was a thirty-year-old woman who shouldn't have to explain her association with a man in his early forties. They were single, consenting adults and didn't need permission or approval from anyone to be out together.

Just get over it, Brynn. Folks are going to think whatever they want no matter if you deny it.

"You're about a six," Evy said, looking her over. "Now, what are looking for?"

"Blouses, a few long skirts and dresses. And one or two belts."

Evy nodded. "Do you mind if I select a few things for you to try on?"

"Not at all."

"You can use the last dressing room on the left, and I'll bring you what I think you'd like."

Forty minutes after entering Cimarron Rose, Brynn walked out with Susanna and two large shopping bags filled with clothes and accessories she needed and some she couldn't resist. She'd also purchased a few pieces for her sisters for Christmas. Silk scarves, cashmere cowls and shawls would go over well with Remi, Corinne and Audrey, and would add to the handmade items she'd planned to gift them.

"I hope Evy didn't embarrass you when she'd mentioned giving you the family discount," Susanna said as she drove in the direction of Bronco Heights.

"I suppose I'm going to have to get used to it because denying that anything is going on between me and Garrett will only fall on deaf ears."

Susanna gave Brynn a quick glance before she concentrated on her driving. "I must admit that you two looked pretty cozy at Doug's."

Yeah right. Garrett had put his arm across her shoulders but that didn't necessarily translate into coziness. "I like Garrett, but we've both agreed to be friends. I know he's divorced, and I don't have the best luck when it comes to relationships, so friendship works for us."

"I never met his ex-wife. The only thing I know is that after they moved to New York, she decided to stay, and whenever his brothers attempt to pair him up with a woman, he's quick to remind them that he doesn't date. He's friendly and outgoing enough, but I'm here to tell you that I've never seen him with a woman. The exception is you, Brynn."

Brynn hadn't asked Susanna about Garrett's ex-wife. If and when he felt comfortable enough with her, she expected him to open up about the woman he'd loved enough to marry. Right now she didn't want to pry into Garrett's personal life, so she changed the subject, asking Susanna how she and Dean met. Judging from the love she'd seen in her eyes when Susanna had looked at her fiancé, she knew it was a subject Susanna would be eager to discuss.

"Even though I'd trained to become an actress, I

had a job working part-time for Abernathy Meats and I liked it there. I was eventually promoted to full-time office manager, and while I'd been dating a few guys, nothing ever came of it."

"Because you'd fallen in love with Dean Abernathy."

She smiled. "I'd been in love with Dean for years, but he'd always treated me like his kid sister."

"When did everything change?" Brynn asked.

"Last year, when I appeared as the lead actress in a Christmas play and my costar had to kiss me. We'd spent a lot of time together rehearsing and Dean went from being the big brother type to becoming a little too overprotective. After a while, he couldn't hide that he was jealous. And that's when I knew we'd become more than coworkers and friends." Susanna maneuvered into the visitor parking lot at the complex. "What's going to happen if you and Garrett go from friends to lovers?"

"Nothing. Because that's not going to happen."

"Is it because it's something you don't want?"

"It's because that's something I don't need. Not at this time in my life," Brynn countered. She hadn't lied to Susanna, and she recalled what her grandmother had warned her about after her last breakup. *Learn to love with your head as well as your heart.*

Susanna shut off the engine. "There was a time when I submitted an application to rent an apartment here and even though it got approved, I decided not to take it."

"Why not?"

"It had been just me and my mother for so many years, I'd felt guilty leaving her alone. I had no idea she was dating someone, and when I met Ted, I knew he was perfect for my mother."

"Good for her."

Brynn thought about her parents breaking up after more than thirty years of marriage. It was as if the Hawkins women were not guaranteed a happily-ever-after. Hattie had lost her husband early during their marriage, and now Josie and Steve were separated, while she hadn't had a relationship of long duration. Obviously, it wasn't in the cards for her to fall in love, marry and start a family. Then she thought about Audrey and Jack Burris. They'd had their difficulties before realizing they were good if not perfect for each other.

Was there hope after all?

She swiveled to her new friend, turning on her positive attitude. "I hope you like Mexican food because I plan to make fajitas for lunch."

Susanna moaned softly. "I love fajitas."

The bond that had formed between her and Susanna at Doug's bar was cemented over steak, chicken and shrimp fajitas, guacamole, and sparkling pink lemonade. Her new friend told her that she'd graduated college with a business management degree and had also added several college productions to her theatrical résumé, but after eight years working for Abernathy Meats she had finally come into her own as manager for the Bronco Theater.

"If you hadn't told me that you had to go to the high school and coach drama students, I would've made margaritas instead of the lemonade."

Susanna's brown eyes twinkled as she laughed. "Margaritas would've gone quite nicely with what you'd prepared. I must give it to you. You're an incredible cook, and I never would've guessed that you were into needlecrafts and fashioning. You should think about opening a shop in Bronco."

While Brynn had been putting the final additions on their lunch, Susanna had lingered in the bedroom she'd set up as her workshop. When she'd emerged, her face had flushed with excitement.

"I've been thinking about opening one, but I'm not sure about doing business in Bronco."

Susanna went still. "Why not?" she asked defensively. "Do you think people here wouldn't want to buy hand-quilted crib blankets that would become an heirloom to be passed down through generations? It would the perfect gift for a baby shower, or a queen-sized one as an engagement gift."

Brynn grimaced. Somehow her friend had misunderstood her. She wasn't dissing Bronco. "There's nothing wrong with Bronco, Susanna."

"Then why are you in quandary about opening a handicraft boutique here? And you would have the option of opening it here in Bronco Heights or in Bronco Valley. Personally, I happen to like Bronco

Valley because a lot of the shops have a funky vibe. Whenever possible, tell Garrett to take you to Sadie's Holiday House. It's gift shop that celebrates Christmas all year long. The instant you walk in, you can smell pine trees and cinnamon, and there's always cheerful holiday music playing twelve months a year."

"That sounds like my kind of shop," Brynn said cheerily.

"It's on the same block as Cimarron Rose, so you can't miss it."

Suddenly, creative ideas flooded Brynn's mind. She was certain she would be able to find the items she needed to add to the ones in her inventory for the festive autumnal wreaths she'd planned to make for the Abernathys.

"You've given me a lot of food for thought."

Susanna patted her belly. "And I've eaten a lot of your food. Thank you for a delicious lunch."

"Any time you want to share lunch, just call and let me know."

Brynn exchanged a hug with Susanna before she walked her to the door. Shopping and sharing lunch with Susanna had been a pleasant way to spend the afternoon. It had been a while since she'd shopped for clothes and most of what she'd selected were for warmer weather, but just knowing they were hanging in the closet if and when she needed something was satisfaction enough. She cleaned up the remains of lunch, and went back to the task of finishing the crib blanket before she began her next project.

HARLEQUIN®
Reader Service

FREE BOOKS GIVEAWAY

YOU pick your books – WE pay for everything.
You get up to FOUR New Books and TWO Mystery Gifts...absolutely FREE!

Dear Reader,

I am writing to announce the launch of a huge **FREE BOOKS GIVEAWAY**... and to let you know that YOU are entitled to choose up to FOUR fantastic books that WE pay for.

Try **Harlequin® Special Edition** books featuring comfort and strength in the support of loved ones and enjoying the journey no matter what life throws your way.

Try **Harlequin® Heartwarming™ Larger-Print** books featuring uplifting stories where the bonds of friendship, family and community unite.

Or TRY BOTH!

In return, we ask just one favor: Would you please participate in our brief Reader Survey? We'd love to hear from you.

This FREE BOOKS GIVEAWAY means that your introductory shipment is completely free, <u>even the shipping</u>! If you decide to continue, you can look forward to curated monthly shipments of brand-new books from your selected series, always at a discount off the cover price! <u>Plus you can cancel any time</u>. Who could pass up a deal like that?

Sincerely

Pam Powers

Pam Powers
For Harlequin Reader Service

Complete the survey below and return it today to receive up to 4 FREE BOOKS and FREE GIFTS guaranteed!

► DETACH AND MAIL CARD TODAY! ▼

FREE BOOKS GIVEAWAY
Reader Survey

1
Do you prefer stories with happy endings?

◯ YES ◯ NO

2
Do you share your favorite books with friends?

◯ YES ◯ NO

3
Do you often choose to read instead of watching TV?

◯ YES ◯ NO

YES! Please send me my Free Rewards, consisting of **2 Free Books from each series I select** and **Free Mystery Gifts**. I understand that I am under no obligation to buy anything, no purchase necessary see terms and conditions for details.

❏ Harlequin® Special Edition (235/335 HDL GRM5)
❏ Harlequin® Heartwarming™ Larger-Print (161/361 HDL GRM5)
❏ Try Both (235/335 & 161/361 HDL GRNH)

FIRST NAME

LAST NAME

ADDRESS

APT.#

CITY

STATE/PROV.

ZIP/POSTAL CODE

EMAIL ❏ Please check this box if you would like to receive newsletters and promotional emails from Harlequin Enterprises ULC and its affiliates. You can unsubscribe anytime.

SE/HW-122-FBG22_SE/HW-122-FBGVR

* * *

Garrett hadn't realized he had been counting down the days when he would see Brynn again until she opened the door to her apartment and he saw her. Everything about her screamed an undeniably youthful beauty that validated what Crosby had accused him of. He was staring at Brynn like a deer in the headlights.

"Are you going to stay there or come in?" Brynn asked.

The sound of her dulcet voice shattered the spell. "I'm coming in."

Brynn stepped aside and Garrett entered the apartment. He handed her a mixed bouquet of fall flowers.

Brynn smiled. "Why, thank you. They're beautiful." She set the bouquet on the edge of the entryway table. Going on tiptoes, she kissed his cheek at the same time Garret turned his head and his mouth landed close to hers. He pulled back awkwardly and started to apologize when Brynn stopped him. "It's okay, Garrett. You can kiss me," she whispered.

Garrett had wanted to kiss Brynn the first time he'd seen her at the convention center, wondering how it would feel to taste her lush lips. It was what he'd wanted to do when they'd sat close together on the blanket during their picnic lunch, and even now it was if she'd read his mind as she challenged him to kiss her.

Looping both arms around her waist, he pulled her close and brushed his mouth over hers, smothering a groan when her lips parted. He tightened his hold on her body, lifting her effortlessly off her feet as he deepened the kiss, their tongues meeting and dueling for dominance.

Garrett could feel the rapid beating of Brynn's heart against his chest, her soft moans indicating she was as aroused as he was. He also he knew that if he didn't stop now, they would only stop when he carried her into her bedroom to demonstrate wordlessly how much he wanted her.

Garrett did not know how Brynn had managed to slip under the barrier he'd erected around himself. He'd been keeping all women at a distance; he'd never wanted to find himself that vulnerable again. But somehow it was different with Brynn.

It took herculean strength for him to end the kiss, and they were both breathing heavily as he set Brynn on her feet.

"That wasn't so bad, was it?" she breathed softly.

"No, it wasn't, but I suppose there goes our friendship."

Brynn lowered her eyes. "You're right. Friends don't kiss each other like we just did."

Cupping her chin, Garrett eased her head up. Overhead lighting shimmered over her delicate features as he stared at her thoroughly kissed mouth. "I know you've probably heard that I don't date."

She nodded. "Yes, I have heard that from a few people."

"Well, that's about to change, but only if we take it slow."

"What aren't you saying, Garrett?"

"Miss Brynn Hawkins, would you be willing to go on a date with me?"

Brynn knew it was too easy to get caught up in the way Garrett was looking at her. She knew her feelings for him were intensifying each time they shared the same space, and while she'd wanted her heart to listen to her head, it had refused. Everything about Garrett Abernathy was so potent and compelling that for her to pretend to be unaffected was futile.

"Yes, Mr. Garrett Abernathy, I am willing to go on a date with you." She smiled when she heard him sigh. "Did you think I was going to turn you down?"

"Like you, I don't like to make assumptions. Other than take you around Bronco, I'd like for you to be my date for an annual charity fundraiser that will be held at The Association the Saturday before Thanksgiving." The event was one of a few held in Bronco Heights, including the popular Denim and Diamonds gala planned by professional party planner Brittany Brandt Dubois and hosted by Taylor Beef owner Cornelius Taylor III and his much younger wife, Jessica, at a massive party tent on their property.

She blinked. "Isn't The Association a private club for ranchers?"

"Yes, why?"

"So, is the event black tie?"

"It is," Garrett said.

"Have you attended the event before?"

"No. This will be my first time."

Brynn was confused. Garrett wanted her at his date at an event he'd never attended. "Why now, Garrett?"

"Because this will be the first year I will have a date. I hope that answers your questions."

"It does for now." She wanted to tell him he really hadn't answered her question. "I suppose I'll have to trade in my jeans for a fancy dress," she teased.

"BH Couture will definitely have something you'd want to wear. I'll call the owner to tell her to send the bill to me."

Brynn recoiled as if she'd been slapped across the face. "If you lift one finger to dial that number, you'll be going to the fundraiser without me. Do you think I can't afford to buy my own clothes for an event?"

"I... It's not that, Brynn."

She stomped her foot. "Then what the hell is it, Garrett? The Hawkinses may not have as much money as the Abernathys, but we're not paupers either. I've been on my own for years. And I don't need a man to take care of me."

Garrett held up both hands in a gesture of submission. "I'm sorry. I didn't mean it like that."

Brynn narrowed her eyes. "You always say what you mean, Garrett."

"I'll admit to that, but somehow, with you, I tend to wind up with my boot in my mouth."

"Why me?"

Garrett smiled, attractive lines fanning out around his eyes. "I don't know what it is, but you tend to keep me off-balance. There are times when I have to rehearse what I want to say to you because I don't want it to come out all wrong. Like it just did."

Brynn couldn't stay angry, not after a confession like that. Her temper cooled and she went on tiptoes again and kissed him. "I'm not really that scary. I'm going to put the flowers in water while you get ready for your second lesson."

"Does this mean I'm forgiven for the faux pas?"

"Of course. There is one thing you should know about me, and that is I don't hold grudges."

"Good to know."

As he chopped onions and green bell pepper, minced garlic, and diced celery and carrots, Brynn noticed that Garrett was much more relaxed in the kitchen than he had been.

"You look like a pro wielding that knife."

"That's because I've been practicing," Garrett admitted sheepishly.

"After a few more lessons, you should be on your own. You already know how to grill steak and burgers. But if you want to change it up and do short ribs, then I'll give you a recipe for a marinade to turn them into Korean barbecue short ribs."

"I like Korean barbecue."

"So do…" Brynn's words trailed when her cell phone chimed a familiar ringtone. "Excuse me, but I have to answer that." She picked the phone up off the countertop and walked to the far end of the kitchen. "Hello, Mom."

"I've got some good news."

"You and Dad are back together?" Brynn saw Garrett turn to look at her when she'd mentioned her mother and father.

"Not yet. But we are working on it. Remember when you were in that Derrick Blackstone video a couple of years ago?"

"Yes." It had been the first and only time she'd appeared in a music video. Josie had gotten the singer's record company to hire her as an extra. Three years ago, Derrick had exploded onto the music scene, turning it upside down with his silky baritone, handsome face and chiseled body. He had won a number of awards as a crossover artist when his songs made the country, pop, hip-hop and R&B music lists.

"I just got a call from his producer, and they want you to appear in his new video. He's covering the Adele song 'Don't You Remember.'"

"I love that song."

"Well, baby girl, this is your turn to shine outside the rodeo arena, because you're going to be the only one in the video."

Brynn felt as if her heart was beating outside her chest. "You're kidding?"

"No, I'm not. The studio will send a car to take you to Billings for the shoot."

"When is that?"

"Right after the Thanksgiving weekend. The shoot has to be done in one day because the single is scheduled to drop a few days later."

"Why me, Mom? I don't think Derrick Blackstone even knew I was on the set when that video was made.

There were so many other people." Brynn knew she wasn't imagining Garrett's glare at her mention of Derrick Blackstone's name.

"He did remember you because his producer personally asked for you. So, try and catch up on your sleep so once you're in front of that camera, the entire world will hold its breath when they see your face. As soon as I hang up with you, I'm going to call the producer and tell him it's a go."

"Wait—" Brynn realized her mother had hung up on her before she could say yes or no. But she knew Josie Hawkins well. Once she latched on to something lucrative, she refused to let it go until the money was in the bank. Her belief was she was put on the earth to take care of her girls and provide for their futures.

Brynn set the phone on a shelf and walked over to Garrett, who was still glaring at her. "I'm going to be in another Derrick Blackstone video that will be recorded at a studio in Billings."

Garrett gave her a long, penetrating stare. "So, you're telling me this isn't your first time working with Blackstone?"

"I didn't work *with* him, Garrett. I was part of a crowd in a bar scene in one of his videos."

"There's no doubt he remembered you in that crowd."

Brynn flinched at the tone in his voice. If she'd known he would react so accusatorially, she wouldn't have shared the news with him. She thought friends were supposed to be happy for each other.

Suddenly she remembered something Susanna

had said about Dean the day she'd taken Brynn to Cimarron Rose. That Dean hadn't realized he'd had deep feelings for her until he'd suspected she had something going on with her costar. A knowing smile flitted over her features. "You're upset, aren't you, Garrett?"

"What are you talking about?"

She decided to press her attack. "You're upset because I'm going to be in a music video with one of *People* magazine's most handsome men."

"That's where you're wrong," he countered, scowling.

"No, Garrett Abernathy, deep down you know I'm right. And you know that there's going to be a lot of talk once people recognize the woman you're dating is in a video with a music heartthrob." She widened her stance and speared him with her dark eyes. "Admit it."

Garrett knew he'd put his boot in his mouth for the second time when he'd questioned Brynn about being in the video. Unaware that he was so transparent, he felt like a complete idiot because she had seen straight through him. He *was* upset. In fact, he was jealous that Brynn would spend hours, if not days, with a man who'd personally requested her for the project.

When he didn't answer, she let out a little laugh and patted his shoulder. "Not to worry, cowboy. Right now, you're the only man in my life." Then she turned to her chopping board.

Garrett stood stock-still, the knife still in his hand.

Brynn may have just admitted he was the only man in her life, but all he remembered was *right now*. Was he Mr. Right or Mr. Right Now? He had to assume he was Mr. Right Now, because he'd made it known that he was too old for her. And as much as he'd tried not to make comparisons between Brynn and Faith, there were similarities that had him questioning whether he'd wanted to go down that road again. Namely, her fondness for city life and always being on the move. He'd showed Brynn how much he loved living and working on the Flying A, and he wondered if she would eventually tire of him and his predictable lifestyle and move on. He'd also broken his promise not to date; however, he'd found himself so emotionally connected to Brynn that he wanted to spend as much time with her as possible before she walked out of his life.

Putting down the knife, he picked up the seasoned oxtail and went to the stovetop.

"We'd better get moving," he said. "The oil is smoking, so it's time to brown the meat."

Brynn gave a chuckle he couldn't decipher, saying, "Yes, chef."

Chapter Eleven

Garrett watched a myriad of expressions on his mother's face as she chewed a piece of fall-off-the-bone oxtail. "What do you think?" As with the chicken-fried steak, there was more than enough for leftovers, and he had given his mother containers with oxtail, rice and smothered cabbage.

Hannah smiled. "It's delicious. I can't believe you made this."

"Not without some assistance. Brynn said this is a Southern version and the next time she'll show me the Jamaican variety. That one has a more intense flavor because of the spices."

Brynn had admitted the recipe came from the *African American Heritage Cookbook*. All were traditional recipes from Alabama's renowned Tuskegee

Institute and had been passed down through count-less generations of Black women.

"You are spending a lot of time with Brynn. Is there something you're not telling me?" Hannah asked between bites.

"I've asked her to be my date for the fall fundraiser."

With wide eyes, Hannah placed a hand over her mouth. "Really," she whispered.

Garrett smiled. He knew he'd shocked his mother. But then, he'd shocked himself when he'd ask Brynn to accompany him because, in a moment of madness, he still hadn't recovered from kissing her. He'd de-cided to attend the event with Brynn to put to rest the innuendos about their involvement with each other; he hadn't missed the looks thrown their way at Doug's or his family's teasing at DJ's. Hell yeah, he liked the beautiful rodeo spitfire, and he thought himself lucky that she wanted to be with him.

"Yes, really, Mom."

Hannah dropped her hand. "Did she accept?"

"Yes."

"I'm so happy for you, Garrett," she admitted, her voice pregnant with emotion. "This works out per-fectly because your father and I plan to skip the event this year. His back is still bothering him, and the doctor wants him to rest for at least two weeks. I'll have him call The Association and let the registra-tion committee know you'll be representing the Fly-ing A. Your brothers have decided not to attend this year, and not having someone from the ranch attend is definitely not a good look." She picked up another forkful of cabbage. "As soon as I finish eating, I want to show you something."

Garrett nodded and shared a smile with his mother across the table. He knew she was relieved that he'd decided to date. Having Brynn accompany him when he attended one of the most fêted events at The Association was like attending the Academy Awards on Oscar night. When Brynn had talked about buying something to wear, it had reminded him that he also had to purchase something more appropriate than a business suit.

If he'd shocked his mother when he'd revealed that he was taking Brynn to the fundraiser, then Garrett was equally shocked when she handed him a flat velvet case that contained the gift Hutch had given her for their recent wedding anniversary. Hannah had been overwhelmed with the diamond earrings and her hands had shaken so much that she'd needed assistance to put them in her ears. They were a mixed cluster of alternating marquise, pear-shaped and round diamonds resembling constellations of brilliant light. Garrett knew Hutch had paid a small fortune for the earrings and had boasted that his wife was worth every penny.

"I'd planned to wear them to this year's dinner," his mother explained, "but because my mule-headed husband is laid up, I want Brynn to wear them in my stead."

He stared at her. "But you've never worn these."

She held up a hand. "Please don't argue with me, Garrett, because I just told Hutch and he agreed with me. He says they are to be worn 'by a woman on the arm of an Abernathy man,' and because you are an Abernathy, then the honor falls to Brynn." Hannah pressed her palms together. "I know you two are going to cause quite a sensation when you show up together."

Garrett narrowed his eyes. "Something tells me you'd like to be a fly on the wall when that happens."

"Don't worry. I have spies that will tell me every-thing."

"Mother!"

"Don't 'mother' me, Garrett. Folks talk and you knew that firsthand when you came back home from New York. I forget how many times I had to shut people down when they asked why you and Faith had broken up. There are just so many ways to say 'I don't want to talk about it' or 'It's none of your busi-ness' before I had to resort to using four-letter words."

"You cussing?"

"Yes, Garrett. I cuss, and I'm pretty damn good at it. Just ask your father. We've had our difficulties over the years, but we've sacrificed a lot to raise our boys and make this ranch a success while always trying to spend quality time with each other. And I can assure you that didn't come often enough in those days. I'm not perfect, and neither is your father, but because we love each other we're willing to compromise. I know it hadn't been easy for you and Faith because you were always going in different directions. Even in your view of having a family."

Garrett had to admit she was right. "I was willing to adopt, and she wasn't."

"You know, she's as different from the Hawkinses as night is from day."

Garrett wondered where his mother was going with this and looked at her with a question in his eyes.

"When I was seated next to Josie at dinner that night, she told me Hattie Hawkins had adopted her and her sisters, and she'd continued the tradition when she'd adopted her two younger daughters."

Garrett's eyebrows flickered. Brynn had told him about her mother and grandmother adopting children. "You two must have discussed a lot of things."

"Things you weren't even remotely aware of, since Brynn had you hypnotized."

He gave his mother a pointed look, wondering how many more times he would have to hear family members talk about his obvious entrancement with Brynn over dinner. Garrett easily recalled how hard he'd struggled not to touch her, not only that night but every time they were together. Touch her in a way a man wanted to touch a woman.

"That's because I like her, Mom."

"Enough to marry her?"

Garrett shook his head. "I can't marry her. She's too young for me." And he didn't add the possibility that she viewed him a novelty, someone she would eventually tire of. Brynn was too used to the bright lights of big cities to be content to live on a Montana cattle ranch. She'd even balked at the possibility of opening a shop for her handmade crafts in Bronco when he knew it would be the perfect location to sell her merchandise.

"You keep telling yourself that and you're going to lose the woman. What is she too young for, Garrett? Too young for you to make love to, or too young to have your babies?"

"I can't believe it," he said, holding his rising temper in check. "You have three daughters-in-law-in-waiting and now you're looking for a fourth? You should talk to Crosby—"

"Crosby's not ready for a relationship or marriage," Hannah interrupted.

"But I am?"

"Yes. But only if you stop lying to yourself. Now, I want you to get out of my house and think about what we just talked about. And take the earrings. I expect to see a picture of Brynn wearing them the night of the fundraiser."

Garrett knew he'd offended Hannah because she'd ordered him out of her home, something she rarely did. He loved his mother and tried not to upset her, but it was as if she failed to understand why he couldn't marry Brynn. He was almost certain Brynn didn't feel the same about him as he did for her.

What he had with Brynn was too new and, although he believed he was falling in love with her, he didn't know whether she even liked him enough to engage in an ongoing relationship that wouldn't lead anywhere. He knew she was scheduled to leave Bronco in December for her next rodeo, and he wasn't willing to predict what would happen to them beyond that. She hadn't even set a date for his next cooking lesson since he'd told her he had to spend more time in the office now that Hutch was temporarily laid up. Was it only his imagination that she'd looked relieved when he'd told her that?

The question echoed in his mind as he drove to his cabin, but he refused to answer it.

Max met him when the door to the garage opened and raced inside. He had left the door to the mudroom ajar and by the time he walked in and removed his boots, the canine had settled down in his puppy bed. He scratched his pet behind the ears. "One of these nights you'll stay and bed down with horses, where it's warm, instead of waiting out in the cold for me." Max gave him what Garrett thought of as the side-eye before closing them and resting his muzzle on the rim of the bed.

Garrett decided to hang out in the basement game room instead of going to bed. The expansive space was where he'd entertained family members. The contractor had installed a mahogany bar wide enough to accommodate six stools. He had a fully stocked bar and a wine cellar with a capacity for sixty bottles. Pool and Ping-Pong tables, leather reclining seating, side tables and a large, wall-mounted flat screen beckoned one to come in, relax and stay for hours.

Going over to the bar, he selected a bottle of bourbon and poured a small amount into an old-fashioned glass. He drank it neat, savoring the smooth, aged liquor with notes of vanilla, oak and caramel on his palate. It was a rare occasion that Garrett drank alone, but this time it was necessary. He needed something to make him temporarily forget that he'd weakened his resolve not to date.

After he'd refilled the glass twice more, he collapsed on the reclining leather sofa and closed his eyes. It was the last thing he remembered until his internal clock woke him at dawn.

Brynn heard the alert ringtone on her phone and nearly panicked. She'd programmed in the notification to allow herself enough time to shop for a dress for the fundraiser. Although she hadn't seen Garrett for several days, they'd exchange good-morning and good-night texts with tidbits about their day.

She'd revealed she was busy with her projects while he'd replied he was equally busy ordering enough livestock feed and supplies to last throughout the winter months, and that all of the vehicles on the ranch were now fitted with snow tires and chains to navigate the deep snow and drifts that would soon be coming. Brynn had sent him two emoticons—a jacket and a face with chattering teeth—along with a message not to forget to stay warm. He'd returned the text with a kissy face.

Brynn showered and dressed in jeans, pullover sweater, boots and puffy jacket, and left the apartment to drive to BH Couture. She parked in the lot, walked to the entrance and, when she opened the door, she was met with the flowery scent of an expensive perfume she recognized but couldn't name.

The boutique screamed upscale. It was the kind of place where, if you had to look at the price tags, you were in the wrong shop. Headless mannequins were draped in couture, which was an homage to the establishment's name. A large triple mirror stood in the back of the shop along with a white leather couch.

"Welcome to BH Couture. May I help you?"

Brynn gave the pretty salesclerk a warm smile. "Thank you. I'm here to find a dress for a formal affair."

Another woman approached them and quietly asked the salesclerk to ring up a sale. Waiting until the clerk had walked away, the woman extended her hand. "I'm Alexis Huntington, owner of BH Couture."

Brynn shook the too soft hand. "Brynn Hawkins. I'm looking for—"

"I know who you are, Brynn. May I call you Brynn?"

She was slightly taken aback that the woman knew her when Brynn had never encountered her before. "Only if I can call you Alexis."

"Please do. And I know why you're here."

"You do?" Brynn wondered if Garrett had ignored her warning not to call the boutique and have them bill him for her purchases.

"Yes. You're planning to attend the fundraiser at The Association with Garrett Abernathy."

Damn! She couldn't believe word had spread that fast around Bronco.

"Garrett called me yesterday to ask if we had any blue tuxedos in stock and I told him we did and that I would put several aside for him. He didn't say who he was taking to the event, but everyone's been talking about seeing you and Garrett at DJ's, and that you two seemed to be really into each other."

Brynn knew Alexis was waiting for her to confirm or deny she was accompanying Garrett and decided on the former. The Abernathy name was legendary not only in Bronco but throughout Montana and they were as recognizable as their name. "Yes, we're attending together."

"Lucky you. You just don't know how many women have been trying to hook him once they discovered he was single again. And it doesn't hurt that he's rich and gorgeous." She waved a manicured hand. "Enough gossip. Now, if you don't mind, I'd like to recommend a gown in a shade that will complement what Garrett will be wearing."

"What color is his tuxedo?" Brynn didn't want them to look like matching mannequins.

"It's called slate-blue aspen and is similar to the color of the blue suits a lot of men are wearing now."

"I was thinking of something in black, but if you have a few dresses in blue hues, then I'm willing to look at them."

Alexis pressed her palms together in a gleeful gesture. "I'm going to love dressing you."

Brynn was ready to pull out every curl on her head when she finally walked out of BH Couture. She'd tried on so many dresses that she'd lost count. Finally, she'd selected a delicate, dark blue, floor-length, black-silk-lined lace gown with a halter neckline. The front slit and décolletage revealed more skin than she was used to exhibiting. But any attention to her chest would be overshadowed by her legs and bared back. She'd found a pair of satin sling-backed stilettoes in the same hue as her dress. Alexis had insisted she also buy a small black evening purse covered with bugle beads and a luxurious, oversized, black-cashmere, silk-lined shawl, along with ultra-sheer navy blue pantyhose.

Two shopping sprees in one week was a first for Brynn. Even when a pair of jeans she'd worn for what seemed like an eternity either ripped or wore out, she loathed replacing them until it was an absolute necessity.

She parked in her assigned spot at BH247 and went upstairs to her apartment. She took off her boots and jacket and went straight to the bedroom to change into something comfortable. The two hours she'd spent at BH Couture trying on clothes had sapped her energy, so Brynn decided working on her projects would wait for another day. After donning a pair of cotton lounging pants and shirt, Brynn hung the garment bag in the closet.

She went into the kitchen, switched on the radio on the countertop and tuned it to station featuring cool jazz. Brynn had just filled an electric kettle with water to make a cup of tea when her cell phone chimed. She picked it up before it rang a second time and activated the speaker feature. "What's up, Audrey?"

"What's this I hear about you going to a fundraiser at The Association with Garrett Abernathy?"

"Bloody hell! Who told you that?"

Audrey laughed. "You sound like a Brit with your 'bloody hell.'"

"I could've said a few other choice words, but I decided not to hurt your delicate ears."

"Don't worry, Brynn. I'd used a few when Jack and I were going at each other. Now, back to Garrett. What's going on with the two of you?"

"Nothing's going on."

She and Garrett had shared a kiss and had agreed to date each other. And he'd indicated he wanted them to take it slow. She'd wanted to ask him his definition of slow. Did he mean slow as in tortoise-slow or slow as in sloth-slow? Brynn would've preferred tortoise, at least it moved faster than the furry large-eyed mammal. Especially because whenever she and Garrett shared the same space, she was reminded of how long it had been since she'd shared her body with a man. She had to admit her self-imposed celibacy was playing havoc with her mental, emotional *and* physical well-being.

"That's not what Brittany Dubois said."

Brynn smothered a groan. Brittany was married to wealthy horse rancher Daniel Dubois, and Brittany's sister Stephanie was engaged to Geoff Burris, while his brother Jack was engaged to Audrey. It was as if she needed a scorecard to keep the names of the couples and their connections straight. She'd been introduced to the event planner when Brittany had attended the Bronco Summer Family Rodeo with her husband Daniel and their toddler daughter Hailey.

"Is Brittany involved in planning the event?"

Brynn asked. If Brittany was, then she would be aware of the guest list and the seating arrangements.

"No. Daniel was just approved to join The Association, and he and Brittany will be attending this year's fundraiser for the first time."

"How did she find out that I was going with Garrett?"

"When I asked her, she wouldn't tell me, but as an event planner she probably has a relationship with the banquet manager at The Association."

"It appears as if all of Bronco will know that we're going together." Brynn told Audrey what Alexis Huntington the owner of BH Couture had said.

"Now that you mention BH Couture, that's probably where Brittany heard the gossip. She just came back from picking up her dress."

"We must have missed each other because I left there a half hour ago."

"Did you find something you like?" Audrey asked.

"It took a while, but yes, I did." She described the gown to her sister.

"Nice," Audrey crooned. "Is it sexy enough to make Garrett drop to his knees and ask you to marry him?"

Brynn did not want to believe her sister had mentioned sexy and Garrett's proposal of marriage in the same breath. "You must be delusional when you talk about me and a man I've known all of two weeks."

"I'm not even close to being delusional, big sis. You can't see what everyone else sees. You and Garrett are like heat-seeking missiles just waiting to combust.

And remember, I've seen you with those other two losers to know Garrett is good for you."

"Good how, Audrey?" Brynn wanted her sister to reveal to her things she wasn't able to discern about Garrett.

"Aside from him being the gorgeous, brooding type, the most important thing is he's a lot more mature than those clowns that weren't worth the time you gave them. And that bronc rider should've been a rodeo clown. I can still remember how he pouted when you won your event and he didn't. And please don't get me started about Miles Parker. He was dumb as dirt if he actually believed he could really keep all his baby mamas a secret."

"It's called hubris, Audrey."

"It's something else better left unsaid. I'm just glad only the family knew you were seeing him."

If Brynn had to say one thing to Miles, it would've been to thank him for keeping their relationship on the down low. "You're right about that."

"Now, back to Garrett," Audrey continued. "I don't think you'd ever have to worry about him cheating on you because I've heard he hasn't been involved with a woman for years before you came along."

Susanna had also revealed Garrett didn't date. As the former office manager for Abernathy Meats, she was more than familiar with the Abernathy brothers. "How do you know this?" she asked Audrey.

"Even though we're new to Bronco, the Burrises and Brandts aren't, and you know folks do talk."

Brynn wanted to say that they didn't talk, they

gossiped. "Maybe he likes being with me because he knows I won't be around that much."

"You keep telling yourself that lie, Brynn, because you're the one that's delusional."

"We'll see who's delusional once we leave for the next rodeo," she countered.

If Garrett wanted to continue to see her once she returned to Bronco, then Brynn was open to the possibility of their making a go of it. She didn't want to read more into her relationship with Garrett because, whenever she'd believed she was falling in love, it never ended well.

"Yeah, we will," Audrey drawled, laughing. "Don't forget to take pictures of what you're wearing. Better yet, I'll ask Brittany to take pictures of you and Garrett."

Brynn chuckled. "You're going to fit in well living in Bronco because, if you're not careful, you'll either become a rumor monger or a keeper of secrets."

"I'd rather become a secret keeper. It's a lot safer than gossiping. The only exception will be my family."

"Thank you, Miss Rodeo Queen."

"I'm not the only queen in this family. Hattie Hawkins was the first rodeo queen, and Mom and our aunties retained the crown before passing it on to you, me, Corinne and Remi."

"You're right, Audrey." She and her sisters had worked hard to maintain the winning tradition their grandmother had established back in the day when Hattie was one of only a few Black women rodeo riders to gain prominence.

"I'm going to hang up now because I've been putting off doing laundry and it's piling up like a snowdrift. Well, as I live and breathe, it's beginning to snow."

Brynn looked out the kitchen window to see flurries. This would become her first winter in Bronco, a town that had a recorded average of forty-eight inches of snow per year. She thought of Garrett grilling in the snow and quickly dismissed the image. Maybe if she gave him a few more lessons, he could cook for himself indoors and stay warmer.

"Talk to you, later, Audrey."

"Later."

Brynn made her tea then, cradling the mug, went into the living room to sit on the love seat and stare out the floor-to-ceiling window at the falling snow, trying to imagine what it would be like to be snowbound with Garrett.

She recalled a rom-com she'd seen where the hero and heroine had been trapped together during a snowstorm and, at the end of two hours, had fallen in love and found their happily-ever-after. However, real life didn't come close to a movie, and she had no illusions that she would find that with Garrett.

Chapter Twelve

Brynn read the message from Garrett and laughed. He'd texted her at five thirty-six in the morning, when she was still asleep. It wasn't until after seven that she'd turned on the ringer to her cell phone to check her messages.

How would you like to go snowmobiling with me this morning before we go Java and Juice for lunch?

She had to give it to him. He was the most unpredictable man she'd ever met.

Yes.

Can you be ready in hour?

Yes.

I'll be downstairs waiting for you.

Brynn opened the bedroom walk-in closet and found the large plastic bin with her windproof jacket, snow pants, gloves and goggles. It had been more than four years since she'd skied. That was in Steamboat Springs, Colorado, when she'd fallen and dislocated her shoulder and had to cancel performing at the Houston Rodeo and Stock Show, which had disappointed many of her hometown fans. Josie wouldn't talk to her for days following the incident and Brynn had finally ended the impasse when she'd promised her mother she would give up skiing until after she retired from competition.

She completed her morning ablutions in record time. She'd styled her hair in a single braid and covered it with a bright-red knitted cap. After putting on the snow pants, Brynn pushed her sock-covered feet into a pair of waterproof sheepskin boots and laced them up. She zipped up her jacket and went down to the parking lot to meet Garrett. He was similarly dressed, all in navy blue, and a ski cap had replaced his ubiquitous Stetson. Standing there against the broad Montana sky, he looked like something out of a magazine. Simply gorgeous.

Garrett pushed off the bumper of the pickup where he'd been waiting for Brynn and stood straight. He smiled when he saw her. He hadn't realized how much he'd missed being with her until now. Somehow she'd managed to fill a void in his life he hadn't been aware was there.

He took a step and pulled her close, lowering his head to brush a kiss over her mouth. "Good morning, beautiful."

She moaned and said, "I could get used to being greeted like this every morning."

Garrett went still. It was the first time since meeting her that Brynn had indicated she had feelings for him that went beyond friendship, other than when she'd asked him to kiss her. "That can be arranged, if that's what you want."

She smiled. "That can only happen whenever I'm here in Bronco, otherwise you'd have to wait for me to come back."

How quickly he'd forgotten how transitory her life was. Here today and gone tomorrow. He couldn't make plans for them to do things together because he wasn't willing to wait for a call from her saying she'd been delayed in some city on the other side of the country.

No, he had to take it one day at a time and not look or plan for anything beyond that. Brynn Hawkins had a life before he met her, and she would continue to live her life once she left Bronco. With or without him.

Garrett didn't want to even think about Brynn leaving Bronco now that he was certain he was falling in love with her. She was everything he wanted in a woman, from her outspokenness, where he never had to guess what she was thinking, to her independence. He admired how she didn't need him or any man to take care of her or to even give her what she wanted. And he suspected the only thing she would need from him was his protection, because he'd been raised to believe women needed to be protected as much as they needed and wanted to be loved.

"How long will I have to wait, Brynn?"

She lifted her shoulders. "I don't know. That will depend on my schedule. But I'm all yours until the Sunday after Thanksgiving. Then I'm off to Billings on Monday and hopefully I'll be back Tuesday."

"Then you're off again in December."

"Yes. I've already told you that."

It was something he couldn't forget. "Yes, you did," he said between clenched teeth. "Let's go."

Brynn sensed a change in Garrett's demeanor that was now as frigid as the outdoor temperatures. He'd gone from loving to distant in less than one point two seconds, and he'd never exhibited that mercurial side of his personality. Audrey had thought of him as brooding while Brynn had glimpsed moments of sadness in his eyes. She wondered if it had come from a divorce he hadn't wanted because he was still in love with his ex-wife.

Brynn knew her feelings for Garrett had changed with not only every day but also with every moment they spent together. And if she had to make a list of qualities she'd want in man she would claim as her husband, then he would be Garrett Abernathy. He was someone she could depend on for everything and that included allowing him to take care of her, which was something in the past she'd believed she didn't need from a man.

She'd been raised to be a strong, independent woman, yet it wasn't easy keeping up that façade. Just once, she'd wanted to become the heroine in a romance novel and have the hero rescue her from all that was seen and unseen. And she wanted that hero to be Garrett.

I want you to always feel safe whenever you're with me, Brynn.

He'd promised her she would always feel safe with him, and she did. When he'd kissed her, she'd known in that instant that he was different from the other men who had kissed her, because it had felt so right and natural to be in his arms. Brynn knew if he had continued the kiss, she would have invited him to make love to her.

She relished in his touch as he helped her into the truck. "Do you have the Ski-Doo in the trailer?" she asked once Garrett drove out of the parking lot. He'd hitched a trailer to the pickup.

"It's a Yamaha, and it seats two."

Brynn felt a shiver of excitement eddy through her. "What's the top speed?"

He smiled. "Whatever it is, I'm not going to test it, Miss Adrenaline Junkie."

"I am *not* an adrenaline junkie, Garrett. Adrenaline junkies jump out of planes."

"You think not, Brynn. Whenever you're on a horse, it's at a full gallop. What's the matter, sweetie? Cat got your tongue?" he teased when she didn't respond. "I'm not going to go any faster than ninety. Will that be fast enough for you?"

"It'll do," she said as she turned to stare out the side window.

Brynn was loath to admit she was an adrenaline junkie because she loved sitting on horse and having it gallop at top speed, between twenty-five to thirty miles per hour. It was when she'd felt most alive, the wind blowing in her face as the landscape whizzed by.

"Where are we going?" she asked Garrett as he headed for the directional marker for the Flying A.

"Further up the mountain trails where the noise from the snowmobile won't spook the bison."

When they finally arrived at their destination, Brynn discovered the air was a lot thinner in the higher elevation. There was also a lot more snow than what had fallen on the city. She watched Garrett open the trailer and attach a ramp to aid in unloading the snowmobile. He handed her a helmet after she'd put on her goggles.

"You can get on the rear seat, and I'll buckle you in," he said after putting on his helmet and gloves.

Her heartrate kicked into a higher gear once she was seated behind Garrett, her arms wrapped firmly around his body.

"Ready, babe?"

"Yes." She was ready for the ride, but not ready for warmth of his body seeping into hers.

The sleek machine roared to life and, within seconds, they were racing down snow-covered trails in a dizzying speed that made everything go by in a blur.

Brynn lost track of time as she gloried in the feel of the air against her face. And despite reaching speeds she'd never experienced before on a horse, she felt safe knowing Garrett was familiar with the terrain.

The sun was higher in the sky when he finally returned to where he'd parked the Ram.

Brynn removed her gloves and then her helmet as she looked up at Garrett. The sun was behind him, and his face was shadowed. Pinpoints of sun had turned the gray in his hair gold, and she noticed this time there was no sadness in his brown eyes; it had been replaced with an expression she'd never noticed before. It was a longing, a tenderness that seemed to reach inside her, and suddenly she wanted to feel the protectiveness of his arms around her again.

She was so wrapped up in her own need for him that she wasn't aware he'd moved closer until she felt the warmth of his moist breath on her forehead. She'd fought her attraction to Garrett and, for the first time in her life, there wasn't that need to win at any course, but rather an urge to give in to what she'd begun to feel for this man. A man she wanted to know inside and out.

Brynn smiled. "I am really enjoying spending time with you."

Attractive lines fanned out around Garrett's eyes when he returned her smile. "That goes double for me. I'd planned to spend the entire day with you, but Dean called me while I was waiting for you to come down, to ask if I would cover the office this afternoon. He's going with my mother who's taking my dad to get an MRI."

"How is your father doing?"

"He's still having some discomfort, and his doctor is recommending the MRI to rule out any possible damage to his spine."

"It's all right, Garrett. We have a lot of time to see each other before I leave for Billings."

A hint of a smile lifted the corners of Garrett's mouth. "Time to do this," he whispered as he took her mouth in a kiss that felt like a caress before he deepened it until her lips parted under his.

Brynn clung to Garrett as if he were her lifeline. She was so caught up in her response to him that she wasn't aware he'd removed her cap and wound his fingers through the braid, loosening it until unbound curls floated around her face and down her back.

It hadn't mattered that they were standing in near knee-deep snow and that the frigid air nipped at their exposed skin. Desire flared to life and threatened to incinerate Brynn as she surrendered to the man and the sensations taking her beyond herself.

I can't! I can't fall in love with Garrett!

She was afraid it would end like the other times she'd believed herself in love. She had to remember to love with her head and not her heart.

A warning bell went off in her head and somehow Brynn managed to end the kiss and practically run to the pickup, open the door and get in. Her breathing was heavy and labored, as if she'd run a race, and she fixed her gaze on the passenger-side window rather than look at Garrett when he slipped in behind the wheel.

"Are you okay?"

She turned to look at him then. What did he expect her to say? She wasn't okay, because kissing him was a blatant reminder that it wasn't enough. She needed more. And the more was making love with him. "I am now."

Garrett hesitated shifting into gear. "What's that supposed to mean?"

"It means I like kissing you."

He sighed heavily. "And I really like kissing you, Brynn, but what I don't want to do is take advantage of you."

"And I'd never allow you to do that." Garrett not treating her as a sex object was one of the many reasons Brynn knew she was certain that, against all her warnings, she was falling in love with him.

Garrett felt as if he were standing on the top of the world with a woman who had unknowingly beguiled him with her strength, beauty and intelligence. He'd tried to convince himself that Brynn was so wrong for him, but somehow she'd checked all of the boxes for what he'd wanted in a woman with whom to share his future.

Not only had she haunted his dreams but also his waking hours. Whenever he'd sat at the desk at Abernathy Meats, he'd found himself unable to concentrate on his work because he couldn't rid himself of the image of her.

He shifted into gear, both hands gripping the wheel tightly to keep from reaching over and resting one on Brynn's thigh. The need to touch or hold her was so intense, it frightened Garrett, and he wondered why Brynn Hawkins had affected him this way and not some other woman.

He managed to push aside all thoughts about the woman sitting inches away when he stared out the windshield at the passing landscape. Crosby had gotten up early to plow the paved roads, and yesterday, because of the forecast of a snowstorm he, Wes and Dean had herded the cattle to a section of the ranch where the mountains blocked snowdrifts and left enough hay for them to eat until they could be moved back to their regular grazing pasture. It wasn't necessary to move the bison as there was enough alfalfa hay to sustain them for days.

"What time do you have to be back at the office?"

Brynn's voice shattered Garrett's reverie. "One." He gave her sidelong glance. "I did promise to feed you, so there's plenty of time to eat and drop you off at home before I have to be back at the ranch."

"We can always order takeout and that way you can get back to—"

"Are you trying to get rid of me, Brynn?"

"No, Garrett."

"Just checking. If I don't get back to the ranch at exactly one, Abernathy Meats will not go under. We do have a full-time office manager who has everyone's number on speed dial if something were to come up that she can't handle."

* * *

Brynn felt and saw heads turn in their direction when she walked into Bronco Java and Juice holding Garrett's hand. It was as if he'd wanted to advertise to Bronco that they were not only dating, but they were a couple. Her hair, which she was usually able to tame with a wide-toothed comb, was now wild, her curls going in every direction thanks to Garrett having undone her braid. She could just imagine what people were thinking. She knew the stunned gazes were from people recognizing Garrett as one of those Abernathys and also that he'd come into the coffee shop with a woman. She'd lived in Bronco long enough to recognize the names of the wealthy ranchers: Taylor, Abernathy, Dalton, John, and Dubois. And although she was familiar with the names, it was impossible to differentiate them from the less well-to-do because they all wore denim, flannel, leather and cowboy boots.

And here she was walking in with Garrett Abernathy, with bed hair, looking as if he'd just made love to her and now needed something to eat to offset the calories they'd burned making love. Brynn didn't want to believe she was thinking about sleeping with Garrett when he was moving so slow she'd shifted him from the tortoise to the sloth category. While she'd given him the say-so when it came to kissing, that would not happen if or when they made love. Garrett would have to initiate it because, if he rejected her, she would be beyond mortified.

"I didn't think this place would be so crowded

considering the amount of snow that fell yesterday," she said to Garrett.

He gave her hand a gentle squeeze as he led her over to table a busser had just cleared and wiped clean. "Things don't shut down in Montana because of a little snow. We put on thermals, dress in layers, and keep on keeping on. Our schools rarely close because of snow."

Garrett seated her and took the chair opposite her. He'd removed his ski cap in the truck and combed his fingers through thick dark hair, giving it a tousled, sexy look. "What do you usually order when you come here?"

Brynn met his eyes across the table. "A chai latte. And either a Reuben or a Cobb salad." She paused. "It's soup weather, but I also want the Cobb salad."

"Why don't you order both? I'll share the salad with you."

"You'll have the salad and what else?"

"I'll order the Reuben, and I'll also share that with you."

"My, my. Aren't you generous?" Brynn teased.

"All you have to do is ask and, if it's possible, I'll give you what you want."

Brynn was startled by Garrett's offer, and she wondered if he'd just said it to pacify her. "I can give myself what I want. What you're going to have to figure out is what I need."

Garrett's eyes grew wide. "What do you need, Brynn?"

She shook her head and willed the heat from coloring her cheeks. "I'm not going to tell you that." There was no way she would tell him she needed him to make love to her.

Leaning back in his chair, Garrett crossed his arms over his chest and cocked his head at an angle. "You're not even going to give me three guesses?"

"Nope."

"I said it before and I'll say it again. You're a cold-hearted woman, Brynn Hawkins."

She laughed softly. "I'm oblivious to name-calling, cowboy. Believe me, I've heard it all."

Garrett lowered his arms. "Are you talking about your exes?"

Brynn nodded. "Yes."

"Do you want to talk about them?"

"Not now. I don't want to spoil what has been a wonderful morning."

"So, it looks as if you're getting used to our wintry weather."

"Let's just say that I'm adjusting to it."

She didn't want to say that being with Garrett had made the difference, that he'd introduced her to things she hadn't experienced before. Like picnics in near-freezing temperatures, and snowmobiling. Brynn knew if she and Garrett did eventually have a committed relationship, it was certain to be unpredictable.

A server approached their table and greeted Garrett by name before she turned her attention to Brynn to take her order first.

"I suppose there's not too many places you can go

in Bronco that people don't recognize you," Brynn said after the woman left to put in their food order.

Garrett flashed a sheepish grin. "It's easy to remember me and my brothers when we all roll up into a place together. And it becomes even more dramatic when our cousins join us. That's when you hear folks say, 'Oh, it's those Abernathys.'"

Resting her elbow on the table, Brynn cupped her chin with her hand. "It sounds like they weren't happy to see you."

"I suppose seeing so many of us together can be a little off-putting."

"I believe intimidating is a better word, Garrett."

"We are hardly intimidating, Brynn. Is that what you felt when you first met my brothers at the Mistletoe Rodeo?"

"No, because they were with their fiancées. But I'm willing to bet if all five of you walked into Doug's, folks would stop and stare."

"It has happened a few times."

Lowering her arm, Brynn wagged a finger at him. "I knew it," she drawled proudly. And she was just as sure it was Garrett's good looks that drew most of the stares.

Garrett wanted to add another positive attribute to Brynn's personality: perceptive. It was obvious she'd been able to discern more about the Abernathys than he had about the Hawkinses.

When he'd first read in the *Bronco Bulletin* that the Hawkins Sisters were scheduled to perform in the Bronco Summer Family Rodeo, he'd gone on-line to look them up. There were a number of articles about Hattie Hawkins and a few about the present-day Hawkins Sisters, but there had been no personal information about them.

But once the news broke that Jack Burris was involved with Audrey Hawkins, it'd created a media frenzy Bronco hadn't seen since Jack's brother Geoff became a bronc rider champion and hometown hero. If Brynn and her family were serious about making Bronco their permanent residence, then the city could boast that they had two winning rodeo families: the Burrises and Hawkinses.

"What's so funny?" he asked Brynn when she turned her head so he wouldn't see her smiling.

"Picturing you Abernathys walking into a place made me think about the saloon scenes in Western movies that begin with a misunderstanding between cowboys and then escalates into an all-out brawl where they wreck everything."

Garrett chuckled. "You've been watching too many old movies."

"I happen to like old movies."

"How old?"

Brynn bit her lip as she thought about some of her favorite films. "For me, they would have to have been made anywhere between forty or fifty years ago."

"I suppose that makes me old."

Brynn went completely still. "Why would you say that?"

"Because you think of forty or fifty as old."

Her eyelids fluttered. "You're not old, Garrett. Not to or *for* me."

Brynn may not think him old now, but what about ten years from now? A lot of people wouldn't blink an eye about him marrying a woman thirteen years his junior, but what if that woman's youthful face belied her age? Even though she was older than Susanna, Callie and Everlee, she looked as young, and there were occasions when she'd reminded him of a fresh-face college student.

The server returned with their lunch order and the topic of age was moot. Although Garrett appeared outwardly relieved that Brynn had not thought of him as old, he still couldn't dismiss the notion that eventually she would prefer someone closer to her own age.

Chapter Thirteen

Brynn felt her breath catch in her throat when she opened the door to see Garrett resplendent in formal attire. A slate-blue jacket with notched lapels and a matching vest. Flat-front, modern, slim-fit trousers. A crisp white shirt with pocket square and a blue bolo tie secured with an inlaid mother-of-pearl and lapis aiguillette. It was the perfect look for the Western-style tuxedo. His usually tousled waves had been tamed by a professional cut and his lean jaw glowed from a fresh shave. His footwear was a pair of black ostrich-skin low-heeled boots.

"You look fabulous."

Garrett stepped into the entryway and closed the door. "I can't believe you've surpassed perfection," he said, ignoring her compliment.

She felt warm all over with the compliment and the way Garrett was staring at her breasts in the revealing décolletage. Several days ago, Brynn had had an appointment at Denise Sanchez's full-service salon for a facial, manicure, pedicure and full body massage, because it'd been much too long since she'd pampered herself. Mrs. Sanchez had trimmed an inch off her hair and, using a blow dryer and large rounded brush, transformed the curls into luxuriously flowing waves that ended at her waist.

However, Brynn decided not to wear it down for the fundraiser, and it had taken her more than an hour to flat-iron her hair and style it in a twist at the nape of her neck with crystal hairpins. Her only allowance for jewelry, other than the pins in her hair, was a pair of diamond studs.

"Well, aren't you a silver-tongued devil," she teased.

Brynn knew it was only the second time Garrett had seen her wearing makeup, but tonight's was much more dramatic than what she'd applied for the dinner at DJ's Deluxe. Smoky eyeshadow, two coats of mascara on her lashes, and a barely there shade of raspberry under the ridge of her brow line matched the blush on her cheekbones and lips. It had taken her a couple of attempts to apply the makeup so it wouldn't appear garish.

Garrett moved closer and handed her something he'd held behind his back. "I'd like you to wear these tonight."

Brynn could not stop her hands from shaking as she took the flat case she knew contained a piece of jewelry. In that instant she recalled the scene from *Pretty Woman* when Richard Gere gave Julia Roberts the diamond-and-ruby necklace to wear to a formal event.

"What is it, Garrett?"

"Open it and see."

Brynn opened the case and gasped when she saw a pair of breathtaking diamond earrings on a bed of black velvet. "I can't, Garrett," she whispered, unable to stop staring at the brilliant stones.

Garrett took the case from her, set it on the entryway table and removed the earrings. "Yes, you can, because Hannah expects to see photos of you wearing them."

"These are your mother's?" There was a hint of panic in her query.

"Yes."

He told her how his mother had planned to wear the earrings to the fundraiser and because Hutch was under doctor's orders to rest, she'd wanted Brynn to wear them.

She removed the studs she wore and replaced them with Hannah's earrings, while silently praying they were insured.

Garrett pressed a kiss to the column of her neck, his cologne wafting to her nose. Not only did he look wonderful, but he smelled delicious. "You're going to be the most beautiful woman at The Association tonight," he whispered in her ear.

Brynn felt like a fairy-tale princess who'd found her real-life prince in Garrett Abernathy. He was mature, confident, gracious, generous, and so blatantly masculine that she had to stop herself from asking him to make love to her.

She met his eyes. "And I feel beautiful whenever I'm with you."

Garrett wanted to tell Brynn that tonight was all about her, and that it had taken more than a decade for him to meet someone like her to allow himself to open up and embrace life. He'd felt as if he could finally exhale the first day he'd returned to the Flying A, but now, since meeting Brynn Hawkins, he knew he'd turned a corner in his life and he was ready to do and share things with her he'd always dreamed of.

He hadn't lied to Brynn about being the most beautiful woman in the room. The dress she'd selected to wear was perfect for her, and Garrett had to force himself not to stare at the soft swell of her breasts rising and falling above the neckline each time she took a breath. She exuded a sexy confidence with her sleek, sophisticated hairdo, dramatic eye makeup, designer garment that showed off her body's curves and long, shapely legs. Not to mention the heels that put her close to his own six-three height.

Garrett groaned inwardly when he saw her bare back as she turned to pick up the shawl off the table and wrap it around her upper body. How, he mused, was he going to make it through the night without making love to her? It wasn't as if the notion hadn't crossed his mind before, but tonight was going to test the limits of his self-control. He knew he hadn't been completely truthful with Brynn or with himself when he'd told her he wanted to go slow. But how much slower could he go when he was aware that her stay in Bronco was erratic? Garrett knew without a doubt that he'd reached a point in their relationship where it had to be resolved.

Brynn picked up her evening purse and house keys. "I'm ready."

He nodded. He was also ready. Ready to embrace the night and the woman he would claim as his for the next few hours.

Brynn exhaled an inaudible sigh of satisfaction when she noticed the bling on the fingers, wrists, necks and ears·of the women clinging to the arms of their escorts. *They ain't got nothing on me. Thank you, Garrett, for insisting I wear your mother's earrings.*

She knew The Association was a private club for wealthy ranchers, and it was apparent their wives or girlfriends, dressed to the nines in haute couture and adorned with precious jewels, had come to be seen. Tonight, there would be no denim, flannel, jeans or scuffed boots.

Garrett gave the women at the registration table his name and received two raffle tickets. He handed one to Brynn. "What is this for?" she whispered as he escorted her into an enormous ballroom with massive chandeliers, where waitstaff were offering flutes of champagne and passing trays of hors d'oeuvres for the cocktail hour.

"There's a raffle drawing for a single winning

ticket and the winner gets to select a charity of their choice. Ten percent of each ticket sold is set aside for a donation."

"Does the charity have to be a local one?" Brynn asked.

"No. There are other fundraisers during the year that are geared to local charities."

Garrett took a flute, handed it to Brynn, then took one for himself. "Here's to a special woman on a very special night."

Brynn touched her glass to his and took a sip of the bubbly. It was an excellent vintage. "Thank you, cowboy, for bringing me one step closer to whether I should or should not put down roots in Bronco."

His eyebrows lifted questioningly. "You are debating whether you want to live here permanently?"

"Well, what do we have here?" came a strong male voice, preempting what Brynn wanted to say.

She turned to find a tall, white-haired man squinting at her before his gaze shifted to Garrett. The woman clinging to his arm, wearing a diamond wedding set on her left hand, was obviously his much younger wife. Brynn noticed his face was flushed with high color and she wondered if he'd had several glasses of champagne.

Garrett nodded at the couple. "It looks like a nice turnout, Mr. Taylor."

"That it does. I think we can temporarily put aside any hard feelings between us so none of that 'Mr. Taylor' business tonight, Garrett. You can call me Cornelius."

Extending his hand, Garrett shook the older man's. "Then, Cornelius it is. Brynn, I'd like you to meet Cornelius Taylor, of Taylor Beef, and his lovely wife, Jessica."

Brynn shook Cornelius's hand and then Jessica's. "It's a pleasure to meet you both." She was more than familiar with the name and Taylor Beef. The Taylors were the wealthiest family in Bronco Heights.

Cornelius squinted at her again. "Aren't you that champion rodeo rider that everyone in Bronco is talking about?"

"You must be talking about my sister."

Jessica patted her husband's shoulder. "Darling, this is Brynn Hawkins. Remember we saw her and her sisters perform at the summer rodeo?"

Cornelius smiled at her. "You're right, dear." He shifted his attention to Garrett. "I don't remember you attending this soiree last year."

"That's because I didn't attend last year."

"As Hutch's heir apparent, you should be coming to all of these shindigs. It looks good for us in Bronco Heights to give back."

Brynn noticed a muscle twitch in Garrett's jaw as he clenched his teeth. It was obvious he wasn't pleased where the conversation with Cornelius was going. She wrapped her free arm around his waist. "Garrett, I see Brittany and her husband. Do you mind if I go and say hello to them?"

Garrett nodded, smiling. "We'll go together. Cornelius, Jessica, it's nice seeing you." He waited until they were out of earshot of the couple before he whispered, "Thank you for the rescue."

"You're welcome." She paused. "Cornelius seems to be a little pompous."

Garrett grunted. "He's a lot more than that, but I'll keep that to myself."

Brittany Brandt Dubois smiled when she saw Brynn and Garrett approach. Brynn had met the event planner at the Burrises's when Brittany had come to eat dinner with her sister's future in-laws. Brynn had also gone with her sister Audrey. Brittany and Daniel were an extremely stunning couple.

Brittany held out a hand to Brynn. "Naomi Campbell has nothing on you, Brynn. You look absolutely beautiful."

Brynn blushed as she pressed her cheek to Brittany's. "So do you, Brittany." The one-shouldered black gown hugged her slender body in all the right places.

Brittany smiled up at her husband. "Daniel, this is Brynn Hawkins. Her sister Audrey is engaged to Jack Burris."

Drop-dead gorgeous Daniel Dubois nodded to Brynn. "I suppose that makes us family."

Brynn nodded. She set her flute on the tray of a passing waiter and looped her arm over Garrett's. "I'd like to introduce you to Garrett Abernathy."

Daniel smiled. "What's this I hear about the Abernathys raising bison?"

"It's true," Garrett said. "I know you breed horses. Do you think we can get together and talk?"

"What about now? That is, if our ladies don't mind us talking business."

"I don't mind."

"Please do."

Brynn and Brittany had spoken at the same time.

Brittany waited until her husband walked away with Garrett's arm over the shoulder of Daniel's tuxedo jacket to whisper to Brynn, "I can't believe you've hooked an Abernathy."

She stared at the other woman like a deer in the headlights. "What?"

"You and Garrett Abernathy, Brynn. I know for certain that your earrings came from Beaumont and Rossi's Fine Jewels because I saw them when my sister Stephanie went there looking for rings once Geoff began hinting about marriage. And if Garrett gave you those earrings, then an engagement ring can't be far behind."

Brynn wanted to tell Brittany that Hannah Abernathy had loaned them to her for the night, but decided against it. Even if she denied they were a gift from Garrett, it still wouldn't stop people from believing whatever they wanted to believe.

She touched her left ear. "They are rather nice."

Brittany gave her a you've-got-to-be-kidding look. "'Nice,' Brynn? What you have in your ears cost more than some people earn in a year. The only thing I'm going to say is the price tag was in the thirty-thousand-dollar range."

Brynn didn't visibly react to the price of the earrings and again prayed that Hutch had had them insured because she didn't want to be responsible for losing them, especially before Hannah had had a chance to wear them.

"It looks as if the Abernathys aren't the only ones spending the big bucks on jewelry." She didn't want to remind Brittany that her eternity wedding band wasn't something she'd picked up at a mall kiosk.

Brittany leaned close. "I normally wear a plain band, but tonight is special. Personally, I think it's tacky to empty a jewelry box in order to flaunt one's wealth."

"It's probably only for occasions like this," Brynn said in defense of the women preening like peacocks.

"You're right, Brynn, because, on an ordinary day, it's hard to tell the Bronco Heights' residents from those in Bronco Valley."

"How do you like living on a ranch in Bronco Heights?" Brynn asked Brittany, deftly steering the conversation away from jewelry.

"I love it. One of these days, you should visit so we can go riding together. Daniel is currently turning a part of the property into a dude ranch as a top-of-the-line resort that will serve an exclusive clientele."

Garrett had promised her that they would go riding on the Flying A, but that wouldn't happen until next month when she returned from the upcoming rodeo. "I'll let you know once I get some time away from performing. And I meant to congratulate Daniel now that he's a member of The Association."

There came an announcement that everyone should proceed into the grand ballroom for dinner, and Brynn waited for Garret to escort her. The ballroom lived up to its name with its marble floors, walls covered in dark green fabric, all set ablaze with light from a grand quartet of enormous chandeliers. And, judging by the green leather chairs at each cloth-covered round table with seating for six, Brynn sensed the room's masculine vibe. Most of the men wore tuxedos or business suits, adhering to the social etiquette of not wearing their Stetsons. A live band was playing easy-listening tunes.

After she and Garrett were escorted to their assigned table, he seated her then himself. He introduced her to the elderly couples at their table, who then asked him about his parents and sent their well wishes for a speedy recovery when Garrett said Hutch was unable to attend this year.

Brynn sat next to a chatty older woman, dripping in diamonds and emeralds, who repeatedly asked her when she and Garrett were getting married. Her response was always the same. They were friends.

White-jacketed waiters stood behind food stations, waiting for a signal to begin serving approximately two hundred invited guests. But first, the master of ceremonies launched the event with a welcoming speech, followed by a benediction. The event planner then had her staff direct tables to the buffet to eliminate crowding.

Brynn, who'd only drank half the flute of champagne, hadn't eaten anything at the cocktail hour because she'd wanted to save her appetite for the dinner. Red meat was in abundance at the carving stations, but she opted for baked chicken and steamed veggies and, when she returned to the table, asked the person with the rolling bar to fill her wineglass with rosé.

Videographers circulated the ballroom, taping the event, which would later be uploaded to The Association's website. There were several photographers snapping still photos of every table, and Brynn was certain her image would be on display with her wearing Hannah's earrings.

This fundraiser was different from a few of the others she'd attended over the years on behalf of the rodeo. There were no long speeches while the attendees complained of hunger before they were served. Music played, conversation hummed, and everyone enjoyed their dinner, until it was finally time for the raffle draw.

Brynn opened her evening purse and took out her ticket as Garrett reached into his jacket's breast pocket for his. The master of ceremonies made a big show of spinning the raffle drum before reaching in and pulling out a ticket. He read the number in a loud voice and then repeated it.

Brynn covered her mouth with her hand. "I have the winning ticket," she said to Garrett.

"Anyone with the winning ticket please come up to the podium."

"Get up, babe," Garrett said into her ear. He rose and pulled back her chair as she stood.

Holding up the ticket, Brynn said, "I have it."

"Then come on up here, lovely lady."

She prayed she wouldn't fall on the marble floor

as she made her way to the podium, and she didn't miss the admiring glances as the slit in the front of her dress displayed her legs from ankles to mid-thigh. The master of ceremonies came down to assist her up the three steps.

She gave him the ticket and he nodded. "We do have a winner. Now, please introduce yourself and let us know which charity you've selected."

He handed her the hand-held mic. "My name is Brynn Hawkins and I've selected St. Jude Children's Research Hospital as my designated charity." Thunderous applause and whistling followed her announcement. As she stepped off the podium, she saw Garrett striding toward her. Smiling, she waited for him to approach and looped her arm through his as he escorted her to their table.

"Thank you."

"No, thank you, Brynn, for being who you are."

She retook her seat, closed her eyes and waited for her heart to stop its runaway beating. She never could've predicted when she'd accepted Garrett's invitation to attend the fundraiser that it would turn out so wonderfully, and she didn't have to have the intelligence quotient of a nuclear physicist to know that his coming to escort her back to their table was a display of masculine propriety. He wanted everyone to know that she belonged to him—if only for that night.

After dessert, when the doors adjoining the ballroom were open for dancing, Garrett touched his napkin to the corners of his mouth and pushed back his chair. "Are you ready for some line dancing?" he asked Brynn when she stared at him.

She smiled. "You dance?"

"Yes." As Brynn placed her hand on his outstretched palm, he eased her to her feet. "Are you okay dancing in those shoes?"

"Watch me, cowboy."

"That's all I've been doing all night, babe, because I can't take my eyes off you, and neither can a lot of these dudes."

She lowered her eyes and never had Garrett seen her so seductive as she was at that moment; he knew if they had been in her apartment he wouldn't hesitate to make love to her. Everything about her was a turn-on, from her head to her toes. And when she'd gotten up to walk to the podium, he hadn't been able to pull his gaze from the seductive sway of her slim hips and bared back in a dress that was designed to make a man weak in his knees. It had done that and so much more. It had set his libido into overdrive.

The live band alternated ballads with a DJ who spun upbeat tunes that had everyone up on their feet. Garrett pulled Brynn close when the Jason Aldean and Carrie Underwood duet "If I Didn't Love You" came through the powerful speakers. The words of song cut like a knife through Garrett and he buried his face in her hair. He felt her heart beat a runaway rhythm against his chest, and he realized she, too, was affected by the lyrics. It wasn't that he didn't love her, because he did love her, with all of his heart. He didn't know how it had happened so quickly, but he was beyond questioning why he needed her.

The song ended and Brynn pulled out of his embrace.

"Please take me home, Garrett."

There was something in her voice that wouldn't let him question her, so he took her back to the table, where she gathered her shawl. He wanted and needed an answer to her abrupt shift in mood, but knew it was not the time to pressure her. He would wait until they returned to her apartment.

The temperature had dropped sharply and while they waited for the valet to bring his vehicle around, he took off his jacket and placed it over her shoulders.

The drive to BH247 was conducted in complete silence, which continued until he escorted her to her apartment. She gave him a sad smile and handed him his jacket. "I'm going to be very busy this coming week, so I'll see you again on Thanksgiving."

She closed the door, not giving him the chance to respond.

"What the…" The curse died on his lips as he tried to understand what had happened to turn what had begun as a special night into a nightmare. Had the song triggered something in Brynn when she'd recalled what had happened between her and an ex? Had she loved the man so much, she'd been emotionally scarred and too afraid to start over with someone else?

Garrett drove back to the Flying A more confused than he'd been in years. He hadn't known Brynn to run hot and cold, but then Garrett had to ask himself if he was that "someone else" when he'd insisted— and not just once—that she was too young for him. Was that the reason she couldn't love him? He knew he hadn't lost her completely since they would see each other again on Thanksgiving. Good thing, because he didn't intend to let her to walk away without knowing if they could try to make a go of their relationship. Or had it already ended?

Chapter Fourteen

Brynn handed Jeanne Burris a large gift bag. "Here's a little something for you that I've been working on."

The Burris matriarch removed the tissue paper and placed her hand over her mouth. "I can't believe you made this, Brynn." She held up the queen-sized, log-cabin-star-designed quilt in shades of blue, cranberry and tan.

"Give Brynn a needle and thread and she can make anything you want," Audrey said as she sat next to Jack on the love seat.

Benjamin Burris walked into the family room to join his family, who had gathered for a Thanksgiving morning breakfast. The high school principal and basketball coach approached his kindergarten teacher wife and ran his fingers over the quilt. "That's some beautiful handiwork, Brynn. This should be exhibited in a museum."

"Most quilts in museum are antiques. I've seen some that were pieced as far back as before the Civil War. There were a lot of quilts that had coded messages for slaves traveling the Underground Railroad on their way to Canada."

"Have you thought about giving lectures about textiles?" Jeanne asked Brynn.

"So says my mother the consummate schoolteacher," Geoff teased, grinning at Jeanne.

"Watch your mouth, son, because there happens to be two teachers in the house."

Geoff held up both hands. "Sorry about that, Dad."

"Brynn doesn't want to teach, but she does want to open her own shop," Corinne piped up. Her sullen attitude had vanished the instant she'd walked into the house to discover Mike had come home for the holiday weekend.

Brynn felt everyone's eyes on her. She'd talked about opening her own business for a while and now that her family was seriously considering settling in Bronco permanently she'd told them it could be a wonderful place to set up shop.

"You better stop vacillating, Brynn, because we've decided we're here to stay," Audrey announced.

She looked at each of her sisters. "So, it's a done deal?"

"As done as a burnt steak," Remi quipped.

"I suppose that means I have to make a decision and real soon," Brynn said. The lease on the apartment she was subletting month-to-month expired in April, and she expected to receive a renewal notice no later than the end of February when she had to inform the building management whether she intended to renew the lease or vacate the apartment. And that meant she had at least two months to say yay or nay.

"What's there to think about, Brynn?" Corinne asked. "You know the Hawkins Sisters always travel together. We can't live here and you somewhere in Seattle."

Brynn frowned. "Who said anything about Seattle?"

"I'm just saying," Corinne countered.

Her sisters were talking about their futures while hers was still unsettled. As unsettled as her relationship with Garrett. He hadn't sent her a text since she'd told him they wouldn't see each other after the fundraiser, and she refused to be the first one to blink. Well, the impasse would end later that afternoon when they went to the Flying A to have Thanksgiving dinner with the Abernathys.

"I don't know about you good people," Jack said as he helped Audrey off the love seat, "but I'm ready to get my eat on."

Everyone got up and walked into the dining room where Jeanne had set out warming dishes on the credenza. And Brynn had to admit she was glad for the distraction. She was no longer on the spot.

Hannah slapped at Garrett's hand when he attempted to pilfer a candied nut from a dish with walnuts, pecans and cashews. "Stop eating them or there won't be any left for our guests."

"You've made enough food to feed the entire NFL," he grumbled under his breath.

"Don't forget we're having the Hawkinses, your aunt and uncle, and their five kids. The last thing I want is to run out of food."

Garrett want to tell her he could never forget the Hawkinses were coming. Especially Brynn. It had been five days since they'd last communicated with each other and he'd found himself keeping busy just so he wouldn't have to think about her. He did double duty getting up early to check on the fence lines, the cattle and the bison before returning to his cabin to shower and head into the office at Abernathy Meats.

"I doubt that's going to happen, Mom. You have two roast turkeys, prime rib, a whole ham, and I don't know how many side dishes." His mother had spent three days preparing for Thanksgiving.

"I need you to play host this year because your father will be spending more time sitting than standing."

Garrett dropped a kiss on his mother's gray hair. "Okay."

It wasn't long till the doorbell began to ring. His uncle, aunt and cousins were the first to arrive, and his brothers and their significant others were close behind. All had committed to bringing dessert and a long table in the formal dining room was covered with cakes, pies, tarts, a tort and a raspberry trifle that appeared too pretty to eat.

The bell rang again and Garrett went to the door to

open it. Several Hawkins women crowded the porch, but he only saw Brynn. She smiled and he returned it and opened the door wider. "Happy Thanksgiving. Please come in."

She gave him two large shopping bags. "These are for your mother."

Audrey cradled a carton to her chest. "There's some liquid libation in here." Crosby arrived in time to take the box from her.

"Corinne and Remi will be here in a few minutes," Brynn said. "They're still unloading the car."

Crosby set down the box. "I'll go and help them."

Garrett met Brynn's eyes. "I should've told you not to bring anything, because my mother has everything covered."

"I don't know how you do it here in the Mountain states, but we in the South were raised never to come to someone's house empty-handed. That shows poor home training."

"Point taken, Miss Hawkins."

She reached into her crossbody bag and took out the case with the earrings. "Please tell your mother thank you for me."

"You can tell her yourself. She's in the kitchen."

Brynn curbed the urge to stick her tongue out at him. Both her mother and grandmother had punished her for the habit when she was child. Eventually, she'd grown out of it. She was grateful when she saw Susanna and smiled at her friend. "Happy Thanksgiving."

Susanna hugged her. "Same to you. Come with

me and I'll show you where you can put your jacket before you meet everyone."

She followed Susanna down a long hallway until she stopped at a walk-in closet that was as large as some New York City studio apartments. She shrugged out of her puffy jacket and gave it to Susanna to hang up.

"Now that I've got you alone, I want to know what's going on with you and Garrett."

Brynn was completely blindsided by the question. "Nothing. Why?"

"He isn't himself." She peeked out into the hall to make sure no one was in earshot. "You can be honest with me, Brynn. I saw the pictures of you and Garrett at The Association fundraiser, and I was blown away by how perfect you are for each other. Everyone said you two looked as if you belonged on some high-fashion runway. And there were a few photos when Garrett was staring at you like you were a dessert he wanted to eat."

Heat flared in Brynn's face. "That's a little graphic."

"Come on, Brynn. We're both grown women."

"Well, I'll admit that I'm not a virgin but—" She stopped herself, not wanting to get into a conversation about sex. Especially not when she had other things on her mind. "What's wrong with Garrett?"

"He's stopped speaking and, when he does, he's monosyllabic. Everyone has been tiptoeing around him and a few times Hannah told him to go home and get himself together because she won't tolerate any of her children grunting at her. I know she's upset because she lost him once when he left the Flying A, and she doesn't want that to happen again."

Brynn felt her stomach drop. "He's talking about leaving the ranch?"

"He hasn't said it outright, but he seems very unhappy."

"What do you want me to do, Susanna?"

"Fix whatever problem you're having with him."

She shook her head. "That's impossible because the differences in our ages will never change."

"That can't be the only problem, Brynn, because, after all, he is dating you." Susanna paused. "Are you in love with him?"

Brynn knew it was futile to lie any longer. She had fallen in love with Garrett. Hopelessly and totally. "Yes."

And she didn't want to tell Susanna that she was a coward. She'd finally admitted to herself on the night of the fundraiser that she had fallen in love with Garrett and that she had to get away from him before blurting it out and embarrassing herself if he didn't feel the same way.

"Something tells me he's in love with you, too. Are you willing to take some sisterly advice from someone who is also in love with an Abernathy man?"

Brynn wanted to tell Susanna that she had enough sisters. But what was one more? "Yes."

"Let Garrett know how you feel about him. If you can't tell him, then show him. And you know what I'm talking about."

"I never figured you for a naughty girl, Susanna," she teased.

"I was a good girl for a long time," Susanna drawled, frowning. "I'd wasted so much time going out with guys I wasn't remotely interested in, meanwhile I kept wishing they would vaporize and then come back as Dean Abernathy."

"It's different for me. After I broke up with my last boyfriend almost two years ago, I didn't go out with anyone until Garrett."

"That's a long time, Brynn."

"It's taken me that long to get over my last ex's duplicity."

"Oh, here you are."

Brynn turned around to see Hannah standing in the doorway. "I want to thank you for the beautiful wreaths. Susanna, can you help Dean hang them on the front doors?"

Brynn waited for Susanna to leave before she reached into her tote and gave Hannah the case with the earrings. "Thank you for letting me wear these. They did attract a lot of attention."

Hannah smiled and put the case into a pocket of her apron. "Just as I knew they would. You and Garrett looked magnificent in the pictures posted on The Association's website. Have you seen them?"

"No. I'll look at them when I go home tonight."

Brynn had forced herself not to look at the photos because she didn't want to be reminded of how that special night had ended. She'd thought of herself as Cinderella dancing with her prince when it had suddenly hit her that she would never have a happily-ever-after with Garrett. He'd believed her too young, and he refused to talk about his ex-wife. He'd asked her about her exes and, although she hadn't wanted to talk about it at that moment, she knew she would if and when she felt the time was right.

"Garrett can show you at his place."

Brynn wanted to tell Hannah that Garrett had never invited her to his house. "It can wait until I get home later tonight."

Her answer satisfied Hannah when she said, "Come with me and I'll introduce you to the other folks in the family."

Brynn left her tote on the floor in the closet and followed Hannah to the family room, where she introduced her as "Garrett's girlfriend" to Hutch's brother Asa and his wife Bonnie. When she turned to look at Garrett, he shrugged his shoulders and smiled. She exchanged pleasantries with Asa and Bonnie's five children who, like Hutch and Hannah's sons, were in their twenties and thirties. Asa had three sons—Billy, Theo and Jace—and two daughters—Robin and Stacy. The resemblance between the ten offspring of the two brothers was remarkable. There was no mistaking them for anything other than Abernathys.

"I see you met another branch on the Abernathy family tree," Garrett said in her ear.

"How many Abernathys are there?"

He smiled down at her. "A lot. We're quite pro-lific."

Brynn returned his smile. "That, I can see. They believe I'm your girlfriend."

"Oh, but you are." He rested at hand at the small of her back. "Are you willing to give them a demonstration?" Garrett lowered his head to kiss her at the same time she pushed him away.

"Stop it, Garrett," she whispered. "You don't have to prove anything."

His eyebrow quirked. "So, you are my girlfriend?"

"Yes."

Brynn noticed Hutch and Hannah smiling at each other. It was apparent they'd witnessed Garrett's attempt to kiss her. And if she was responsible for getting Garrett out of his funk, then it was a day to be grateful for many things.

Garrett, sitting next to Hannah, found himself listening more to the conversation floating around the table than concentrating on the food on his plate. Hannah had placed two leaves in the large rectangular table to seat twenty-two adults and Maeve and Lola. Plates overflowed with food and glasses with wine as the merriment continued, much to the delight of Lola and Maeve who had come down with a case of the giggles.

He had purposely sat across the table from Brynn to watch her interact with his cousins, who seemed as taken with her as he was. He'd missed her. Not seeing her text messages had left him in a funk where he'd found himself at odds with everyone who questioned him about Brynn after they'd seen the photos of them together at the fundraiser. And rather than lie about what had become a very fragile relationship, he'd stopped responding at all, with the hope people would stop asking.

Garrett had managed to apologize to his mother because he knew she was concerned that he was spending so much time alone again. He got up early to do his chores, then retreated to the office for a few hours to take over from his father, who'd returned to the office part-time, before heading to his cabin. Now that most of the snow had melted, he spent time exercising Tecumseh and trying to saddle train Chief Joseph. However, the colt resisted each time he attempted to put a saddle on him, so Garrett had decided to leave that task to Dean, who had become the Flying A's horse whisperer.

He noticed his mother resting her head on Hutch's shoulder as she struggled to keep her eyes open. The strain of cooking for days had taken its toll. "Mom, why don't you go and put your feet up? We can take care of everything here."

She opened her eyes and smiled. "It's okay, Garrett. Callie, Susanna and Evy have volunteered to clean up and put things away."

"Are you sure?"

She nodded. "Very sure. Now, it's time you make up with that girl or so help me I'll disown you."

"I'm going to talk to her."

"When, Garrett?"

"Later. After we finish dinner."

"That may be too late. I overheard Audrey say

they're going to the Brandts' for dessert after they leave here."

Garrett forced himself not to panic. He knew if he didn't talk to Brynn tonight, he wasn't certain when he would get the opportunity again. He rose, walked around the table and leaned over her, ignoring those staring at him. If they thought he was acting crazy, then he was. Because he was crazy in love with Brynn Hawkins.

"I'd like to talk to you," he said in her ear.

She stared over her shoulder. "Now?"

He nodded. "Yes, please."

Brynn felt like a specimen on a slide as everyone sitting around the table watched Garrett pull back her chair. She wanted to ask him why he couldn't wait for everyone to finish eating before making her the center of attention.

"Excuse me," she said to the table.

"Where is Uncle Rhett going?" Lola shouted.

Evy rolled her eyes and shook her head. "It's okay, baby girl. Your uncle needs to take care of some business."

"With his girlfriend?" Lola asked.

The entire table erupted into laughter as Brynn followed Garrett out of the dining room. "Where are you taking me?" she asked.

"I want you to get your coat because we're going outside."

"Outside to do what, Garrett?"

"Talk, Brynn. I've had enough of my family ingratiating themselves in what's going on between us."

She gave him a sidelong glance. "Maybe they're concerned because you haven't been the nicest to be around."

"Oh. You've heard about that?"

"Loud and clear, Garrett. And I don't want your family to blame me for your bad moods."

"They're not blaming you for anything. They're blaming me for our breakup."

Brynn stopped and gave him a long, penetrating stare. "Our breakup? You're breaking up with me?" Her heart picked up its pace and, despite the chilly evening, her palms began to sweat. Was he trying to tell her he didn't want to see her anymore?

"You broke up with me."

She shook her head, feeling confused and scared at the same time. "No I didn't."

"Then what the hell was going on this week when you said you couldn't see me?"

"I told you I was busy, Garrett. I needed to make the door wreaths as a house gift for your mother—"

"Why didn't you say that?" he interrupted.

"I told you that, Garrett. I shouldn't have to dot every *i* and cross every *t* when I say something to you. I went through that with another man, and I swore I would never do that again." What she couldn't tell him was that she had fallen in love with him, believing if she were able to put some distance between them her feelings would change. Unfortunately, they hadn't. Seeing, talking, and sharing the same space had proven her wrong.

"Please get your coat and your bag because it appears as if we need to talk about a lot of things."

Brynn retrieved her coat and tote, and followed Garrett as they left the house through a rear door. It was a beautiful, late-fall night, with a near-full moon and a cloudless sky sprinkled with millions of stars. She sucked in a lungful of crisp air, held it for several seconds before exhaling.

"Now I know why Montana is called Big Sky Country. It's beautiful."

"And yet you want to leave it."

He began walking, and she sped up to fall in step with him. "Who told you I'm leaving?"

"You did in so many words, Brynn. When I asked you about opening a shop in Bronco, you said that wasn't a possibility."

"That was before my family finally agreed they want to settle here permanently."

He stopped and held her shoulders. "What are you saying? You're staying in Bronco? It's a done deal?"

Was she staying? Brynn needed a moment to sort out her thoughts and emotions. It didn't take her long. She looked at Garrett and shook her head as her lips turned up in a slight grin. "It's as done as a burnt steak. And that's a quote from Remi." There wasn't any question left. She could never leave her sisters.

Garrett picked her up and swung her around and around until she pleaded with him to stop. He did stop, still holding her off her feet, and brushed his mouth over hers, increasing the pressure until her lips parted. The kiss was gentle, healing, and in no time she felt desire course through her veins. Everything about the man holding her to his heart fed a need and filled a void she wasn't aware had existed.

Looping her arms around his neck, she breathed a kiss under his ear. Susanna's advice echoed in her head. *Let Garrett know how you feel about him. If you can't tell him, then show him.* She screwed up her courage and asked him, "Now that I know what *I'm* doing, I have to you ask you, Garrett. What are *we* doing?"

He eased back and set her on her feet. "What are you talking about?"

"Are we ever going to be together?"

He hesitated and she could see his Adam's apple bob as he swallowed hard. "I don't want to make a mistake, Brynn." He said it without looking at her.

"What are you talking about?"

"Making love with you." This time his rich brown eyes gazed directly into hers.

She blinked. "You believe our making love will be a mistake?"

"I don't know."

"What I do know, Garrett, is the only mistake is for us to miss this opportunity. Once I'm back on the road, I'm not certain when I'll be back. But it's not going to be forever because I'm thinking of buying property here. Nothing elaborate or fancy. Just a little house with enough land for me to build a workshop."

"What about horses?"

"That will come later and only if the property is large enough."

Brynn was staying in Bronco. She was buying property and setting down roots. Garrett felt as if a weight had been lifted off him. He didn't want to lose her because he not only wanted her, he needed her. Cradling her face, he pressed a kiss to her lips. "You have no idea how much you mean to me."

"I'm beginning to suspect that I mean a lot to you."

"Your suspicions are correct," he whispered. "I'm a little bit crazy about you, Brynn Hawkins." Garrett had said "crazy" when he'd wanted to tell her he loved her.

"You need to show me how crazy you are, Garrett Abernathy."

The sassy, outspoken woman with the beautiful face and body to match had just challenged him, and he was never one to back down from a challenge. "I would, but I'm sure your sisters are waiting for you."

Reaching into her tote, Brynn took out her cell phone and sent a group text telling them she was staying on at the Flying A and they should go to the Brandts' without her. She showed Garrett the text. "Now, are you going to make a liar out of me? I want to go home with you."

Garrett combed his fingers through her soft curls. "You can't imagine how long I've waited for you to say that. The first time I brought you to the ranch, I thought it strange that you didn't ask to see my home."

"Maybe I was waiting for an invitation."

"Well, then, Brynn Hawkins, will you come home with me now?" he whispered against her moist lips.

Chapter Fifteen

Brynn didn't know what to expect, but it wasn't the large log-and-stone cabin built on a bluff with views of the mountains in the distance. Holding her hand, Garrett told her the house was mostly constructed of salvaged timbers and reclaimed wood and stone. Sturdy timbers, a cathedral ceiling, and a wall of stone with a wood-burning fireplace played up the scale of the great room. A leather sectional grouping and area rugs in muted shades of brown, tan and gold added to the coziness of the yawning space.

"How many rooms are in this house?" she asked as she climbed the staircase with Garrett.

"Four bedrooms, three bathrooms on the second floor. There's another bathroom in the basement game room and a half bath off the kitchen."

Brynn wondered if he'd built his house for his ex-wife with the expectation it was where they would raise their family, because it was obviously much too large for a man living alone. Their footsteps were muffled in the deep pile of the rug along the second-floor balcony with unobstructed views into the heart of the house.

Garrett led Brynn into his bedroom and turned to face her. He knew, once he made love to her, there would be no turning back. No more talk about his not dating or his insistence they remain friends. He met her steady gaze and wondered if she knew how special she'd become to him. She was the first woman other than family he'd invited into his home, and he wanted her to be the last. Since meeting her, every other woman he'd met or known had ceased to exist. He still didn't know what there was about her that turned his life upside down where she had become as essential to him as breathing.

He couldn't predict where their relationship would lead, but Garrett had resigned himself to take it day to day. He had the Flying A and Abernathy Meats, while Brynn was a part of a troop of riders performing in rodeos all over the country. But then there was her plan B as a crafter that would become her sole focus once she retired as one of the Hawkins Sisters. And how long it would take before she would give up her nomadic lifestyle was a question he believed she wasn't prepared to answer.

Don't overthink it. Just accept the right now and

let tomorrow take care of itself. You're about to make love to a woman who ensnared you in her web the instant your eyes met, and now all of your fantasies are about to become a reality.

Garrett took his time undressing Brynn as he removed her blouse and then a delicate camisole to reveal a white lace bra. Anchoring his hands under the straps, he pushed them down and visually feasted on her firm breasts above a narrow waist he could span with both hands. Breasts that he'd only glimpsed the night she'd worn the sexy dress with the plunging neckline and slit that revealed a pair of long legs that seemed to go on forever in the heels that had added at least four inches to her graceful, statuesque body.

She closed her eyes, moaning as he took one breast into his mouth and suckled her before shifting attention to the other. His fingers caught her hair, holding her head in a soft but firm grip as he rained kisses along the column of her neck before he covered her mouth with his, his tongue simulating making love to her.

Brynn felt as if she were drowning in a quicksand of passion that slowly sucked her under when Garrett undid the waistband on her jeans and his hand searched between her thighs to find her wet and pulsing with a need only he could assuage. Her hands were as busy as his, unsnapping his shirt and pushing it off his shoulders before they undid his belt to relieve him of his jeans.

Everything ceased to exist for her as she lay naked

on Garrett's bed, watching as he shucked his jeans and briefs and then reached into the drawer of the bedside table for a condom. He slipped it on his erection, their eyes meeting before he turned off the lamp, plunging the room in darkness.

His mouth charted a course from her lips to the soles of her feet, tasting and feasting on her body. Garrett had become sculptor as his fingers skimmed her curves before he took her mouth again. Brynn moaned at the same time she whispered that she wanted to feel him inside of her.

Garrett entered her and that single overwhelming motion threatened to shatter Brynn into a million pieces. He seemed to know when she was ready to climax, and changed rhythm, leaving her poised on a precipice with nowhere to go. He'd stopped her orgasms twice and, when she couldn't bear the buildup of passion any longer, he freed her and himself in an explosion of sensations. In that moment, she had to bite her lip to stop from confessing how much she loved him.

They lay together, legs entwined, waiting for their respiration to return to normal. Garrett had taken her to heights of passion Brynn had never experienced before. He'd awakened a response deep within her that was incredibly powerful and, if she had to admit, a bit frightening.

Garrett loathed pulling away from Brynn's warmth but knew he had to get out of bed and discard the condom. He'd never had a woman respond to his lovemaking like Brynn. She'd held nothing back.

He'd known he had fallen in love with Brynn before sharing a bed, and now after making love he knew he couldn't let her go. Everything about her was imprinted on his brain like a permanent tattoo: her taste, smell, the texture of her silky skin, her soft moans of sensual pleasure, and how their bodies were in exquisite harmony when they'd climaxed together. Garrett instinctually knew he would never tire of making love to and with her.

He kissed her throat, smiling. "I'll be right back."

Brynn moaned. "Don't take too long."

He kissed her mouth. "I won't."

Slipping out of bed, Garrett walked on bare feet to the en suite bath. He dropped the condom in a wastebasket, switched on the night-light outside the bathroom, and returned to the bedroom to find Brynn lying on her side, the sheet pulled up around her shoulders. He adjusted the thermostat, raising the temperature in the room, and got in bedside her and settled a blanket over her.

Brynn woke disoriented and felt the heat from the body next to hers. Lying in bed with Garrett felt as if she'd finally found her home. She turned and was able to make out his form in the glare of the nightlight outside the en suite bathroom. Decadent as it might be, she let her eyes study him, slowly, taking in every inch of him. He lay on his back, one arm over his head, his smooth chest rising and falling in an even rhythm. His clothes had concealed a lean yet muscled body that hadn't come from his spending hours sitting at a desk or working out at a sports club. No, Garrett's physique came from lifting two-hundred-pound bales of hay. And it was perfect.

She was startled from her exploration when he began tossing and moaning and Brynn realized he was having some kind of dream. He woke, sat up and, with wide eyes, stared at her. "Are you all right?" she asked. He sighed and nodded. "What were you dreaming about?"

"Nothing. I don't remember," he added as he lay back again and pulled her against his chest. "Go back to sleep."

Resting her head on his shoulder, Brynn didn't believe him. He'd been sleeping peacefully and whatever he'd been dreaming about had been disturbing enough to jolt him awake. After a while, she did go back to sleep and then woke to find Garrett leaning over her.

"What time is it?"

"Five thirty."

"That early?"

"When you live on a ranch, five thirty isn't early. I have to take care of some chores around the ranch, but you're welcome to stay until I come back."

"Where am I going, Garrett? I can't walk back to my apartment." She'd come to the ranch in Audrey's SUV.

"I'll be back around lunchtime, then I'll drop you

at your place for you to change your clothes. It's Black Friday, so I suggest we do a little Christmas shopping."

"I like the sound of that."

He kissed her. "I was hoping you would say that."

Brynn lay in bed after Garrett left, wondering how it would feel to wake up beside him every morning. She didn't want to think about marriage, because she knew it was something neither of them was ready for. She finally got out bed and went into the bathroom, where she discovered a drawer with a supply of toothbrushes and travel-sized toiletries.

Twenty minutes later, she emerged from the bathroom, her hair falling around her face like curling wet ribbons. She'd looked but hadn't found a shower bonnet. Brynn went to her discarded clothes on the chair and put them on. She looked around the bedroom and sitting area, thinking it really needed a woman's touch. She wondered how many women had slept with Garrett in the same bed where she'd lain with him, then realized she had no right to feel jealous. She'd been the one to ask Garrett to bring her to his home and make love to her.

She made the bed and then went downstairs to see if she could find anything in the refrigerator to sustain her until she and Garrett had lunch. Brynn had just opened the refrigerator when she heard a knock on the front door. She went to see who it was and gasped when she saw Garrett's mother. Her smile belied the turmoil roiling in her when she opened the door. "Good morning, Mrs. Abernathy."

"I think it's time you call me Hannah. I know Garrett is out working, so I thought I'd bring you some coffee and muffins."

Brynn stepped aside to let Hannah enter. It was apparent her awkwardness was for naught because no doubt it was something Hannah did whenever her sons entertained women in their homes.

"Come into the kitchen with me so we can talk," Hannah said. "I made enough muffins for us to have a couple and leave a few for Garrett. I had some leftover Granny Smiths, so I decided to bake muffins this morning."

"Aren't you exhausted from all the cooking you did to host that feast yesterday?"

Hannah took down cups, saucers and dessert plates from an overhead cabinet. "I admit I was a little pooped, but after a good night's sleep, I'm raring to go again."

"I don't know where you get the energy."

"When you're a mother with five kids, you're imbued with an energy you didn't know you were capable of."

"But your sons are adults."

Hannah waved a dismissive hand. "Once a mother, always a mother. Even though all of our sons have homes of their own, they still come by the main house to check on what I'm cooking."

Brynn smiled. "It was the same with me and my

grandmother. Growing up, I spent more time eating in my grandmother's kitchen than I did in my mother's."

Hannah poured coffee into the delicate china cups from a large thermos. "I know you're a good cook because Garrett gave me some of the oxtail stew, rice and smothered cabbage you had him make, and it was delicious. I'm glad you brought some light into Garrett's life. It's been a long time since I've seen him looking so happy. Ever since Faith did a number on him."

A slight frown appeared between Brynn's eyes. "He had a religious crisis?"

Hannah went still. "Garrett has never mentioned his ex-wife Faith?"

"No."

"Well, that's water under the bridge now that he's involved with you."

"What happened between them?"

"It's not my place to say. But it happened a long time ago and Garrett is over it. You may not want to believe it, but Garrett is in love with you, and that's all that matters." Hannah opened the fridge and took out a container of cream. "Do you want cream or milk?"

"Cream is fine."

Brynn sat at the breakfast island with Hannah, listening to her talk about some of the stunts her sons had pulled on her when they were younger as she munched on the delicious apple-filled muffins and sipped the fragrant coffee with a hint of hazelnut. It felt so natural talking with Garrett's mother that she'd completely forgotten the awkwardness of the situation—having breakfast with the mother of the lover she'd spent the night with.

Garrett returned to the cabin around noon and found Brynn sitting on the floor with Max. The dog had gone out with him earlier that morning and then, a few hours later, he'd returned to the house.

Brynn looked up. "He was on the porch barking, so I let him in. Is he allowed in the house?"

Garrett smiled. "If he wasn't, then it's too late now. Yes, he's allowed in the house. But I don't need you spoiling my dog." She could see him trying to stifle a laugh as he looked at Max laying on his back, eyes closed as Brynn rubbed his belly.

"A little belly rub will hardly spoil him."

Garrett took off his corduroy jacket and pulled a waffle weave shirt over his head. "If he turns into a mush, then he's yours."

Brynn stared at his sculpted upper body, hoping Garrett wouldn't see the lust in her eyes. "I don't think I'm allowed to have pets in my apartment complex."

"Then you'll just have to move in here to take care of him."

Her fingers stilled in the soft, thick fur. Did he say that as an offhanded invitation for her move in with him? Or was it in jest? She decided on the latter.

"Once I buy my house, I'll definitely adopt him." She stood and Max rose, too. "Your mother stopped by this morning with muffins and coffee. And we…" Her words trailed off before she could tell him they'd had a conversation about his ex-wife. It was obviously a sore subject for Garrett if he never talked about her.

"What were you going to say?"

"It's nothing. I'm ready to go back to my place after you shower and change. I figured we could stop at Bronco Brick Oven Pizza for lunch. My treat."

"Are there any leftover muffins?"

"Of course, Garrett."

"I'm going to wash my hands and grab one before I go upstairs and shower. Right about now, I'm hungry enough to eat half a cow."

Brynn stared at the way Garrett's jeans hugged his behind and thighs as he walked out of the great room toward the half bath off the kitchen. He was the personification of sexy coming and going.

Garrett drove Brynn to her apartment, waiting in the living room for her to change; he'd suggested she pack a bag with enough clothes to last the weekend. He wanted them to spend as much time together as possible before she left to go to Billings for the Derrick Blackstone video shoot.

He still was attempting to wrap his head around the fact that the woman with whom he was sleeping was going to appear in music video with a man whose reputation as a player preceded him. Women of all ages vied to get his attention, and it was on a rare occasion that Derrick Blackstone had attended an award show without a beautiful woman clinging to his arm. And there was no doubt he'd noticed Brynn in the crowd of extras during one of his videos. What man wouldn't?

Brynn emerged from her bedroom dressed in a pair of black jeans, a black watch blouse, a green pullover sweater and black leather booties. She handed him a quilted bag and then slipped her arms into a black-suede, fleece-lined, three-quarter coat.

"You look nice."

She smiled and set a black Stetson on her head. "Thank you."

Garrett tugged on the single braid falling down her back. "You're welcome."

"Let's go, because I can hear your belly making noises," she teased.

"Normally I would've gone to the main house to eat because I know there's tons of leftovers, but I had someone at home that it was impossible for me to ignore," he said, smiling.

"If I'd had a vehicle, I could've driven over to where you were working to bring you something to eat."

Garrett waited for her to lock the door. "You would have?"

"Of course, I would have. If you're spending hours working outdoors, then you'd deserve to take a break to eat something."

That was something he'd wanted Faith to do but she'd refused to venture any further than the main house because she'd claimed the smell of cow manure made her nauseous. In reality, she had resented him not building a house for her on the ranch. The first two years of their marriage, they'd lived in his wing of the main house, and he had promised her once they had a family he would build her dream house. He didn't regret that hadn't happened.

"That's nice of you to offer."

"It has nothing to do with nice, Garrett. It's being considerate."

"Well, not all people are generous or considerate, Brynn."

"That depends on how they were raised,"

Garrett helped her up into the pickup. "This is the second time you've mentioned that."

"That's because it's everything," she said as he got in and sat next to her. "Folks usually act a fool when they don't have any home training."

He tapped the start button and drove out of the parking lot. "That's what my parents, aunts and uncles used to say to us whenever their kids got together. 'Don't forget that you are an Abernathy' and 'Don't do anything to disgrace the name.'"

"I noticed that you and cousins seem really close."

"That's because their ranch is close by and we've all grown up together."

"Are any of them married?"

"Nope."

"What are they waiting for, Garrett? There are a lot of single women in Bronco."

"I suppose when they meet that special woman, then they'll settle down with a wife and kids."

Garrett remembered when some of the boys at his high school were proposing to their girlfriends and then married them a year later, becoming fathers before they'd celebrated their twentieth birthday.

He maneuvered into the last remaining space within walking distance of the Bronco Brick Oven Pizza lot.

The city was decked out in holiday decorations with garland draped across most store windows, while city workers in cherry pickers were affixing plastic wreaths, nutcrackers, snowmen and holly to lampposts. Planters on the sidewalks, usually overflowing with ivy, were now filled with red, white and green poinsettias. There were Christmas lights everywhere, and signs announcing the annual tree lighting to be held the first Saturday night in December. Every year the citizens of Bronco and many from nearby towns attended the festive tree-lighting event.

Sidewalks were crowded with shoppers looking for Black Friday sales, and when he and Brynn walked into the pizza shop, they were told there would be a twenty-minute wait before they would be seated.

"Do you want to wait?" Brynn asked him.

"I don't mind waiting. I'm willing to bet every place in town is crowded because it's Black Friday and everyone's out shopping."

They were eventually showed to a table and, after fortified with three slices of pepperoni pizza to Brynn's one slice of white pizza, Garrett headed for Bronco Valley.

Brynn felt as she'd been transported to the fictional Santa's workshop at the North Pole when she walked into Sadie's Holiday House. She drew in a breath and smiled as the scent of cinnamon and pine trees wafted to her nose. Even if she hadn't been in the holiday spirit, she was now. She recognized the distinctive baritone voice of Bing Crosby singing "White Christmas" coming from speakers.

"This place is amazing," she said, looking at the rooms of decorations. "Even better than FAO Schwarz at Christmastime."

Garrett chuckled. "That's really saying something." Then he went off to look at an item that had apparently caught his eye.

She was busy perusing a collection of nutcrackers, humming under her breath along with the song, when she heard a voice behind her.

"May I help you with something?"

Brynn turned and smiled at a young woman with long, wavy, blond hair and brown eyes with long, thick lashes. "I don't know, because there's so much here that I'm ashamed to say I'm a bit overwhelmed."

"I'm Sadie Chamberlin, the owner of this year-round holiday-themed establishment." When Brynn introduced herself, Sadie asked, "Is there anything in particular I can help you find?"

Brynn glanced over at Garrett, who was busy with a pair of nesting dolls. "I know I want to get a nutcracker for one of my sisters, because she began collecting them a few years ago."

Sadie indicated the table in front of her. "Well, you're in the right place. And just to let you know, everything you see is for sale, and that includes the decorations. Each of the rooms on the first floor has a holiday theme. One is for Hanukkah, decorated in blue, white and silver, and another for Kwanzaa in red, black and green."

"What's upstairs?"

Sadie eyelids fluttered as she bit her lip and Brynn wondered if she was okay.

"Everything you need to decorate from New Year's to Thanksgiving."

Garrett, carrying a nesting doll, joined them. "Hello, Sadie."

"Hi, Garrett. You two make a good couple."

Garrett put his free arm around Brynn's waist and she was helpless to stop the rush of heat suffusing her face. He thanked Sadie, and asked if she could recommend gifts for a two- and four-year-old. Brynn noticed that Sadie appeared distracted as she helped her and Garrett pick out gifts for their families.

"I'm sorry if I'm a little out of sorts," Sadie apologized as she tallied their purchases. "Rumors are swirling again that my former brother-in-law, Bobby, is alive and lurking around Bronco."

Garrett handed Sadie a credit card. "Folks have been talking about seeing Bobby Stone around Bronco for a while now." He shrugged. "I guess it's true what they say…everyone has a doppelganger."

"I know," Sadie said, "but it's unnerving because different people have told me that they've seen him." She tapped Garrett's card on the reader and then returned it to him before she filled two shopping bags with their purchases.

Brynn took one of the bags. "Thank you."

A nervous smile flitted over Sadie's mouth. "I'm glad I was able to help you. It's nice seeing you again, Garrett."

He nodded. "Same here, Sadie."

"How often do you shop here?" Brynn asked Garrett as they made their way to the door. Before he could answer, the door opened and a tall, good-looking man walked in. From behind them, she heard Sadie let out a strangled cry and she turned to see the shop-keeper collapsing to the floor.

Garrett, she noticed, stared at the man who'd swept passed them and now knelt beside Sadie. "Bobby?"

The man Garrett had called Bobby glanced at him over his shoulder, shaking his head. "No. But I understand why you might think that."

They rushed back over to Sadie, who lay on the floor, coming to. As she opened her eyes, she reached up to touch the face of the man hovering over her. "Bobby? Is it really you?"

The man shook his head. "I guess we really do look the same." He helped Sadie to a sitting position and Garrett asked if they should call someone for her. Sadie declined, but her eyes never wavered from the stranger.

Once they were sure she was all right, Garrett reached for Brynn's hand. "Let's go and let them sort this out."

Brynn heard Sadie and the man talking as she and Garrett left the shop, but she couldn't make out their words. "That was weird," she said when they stood outside the shop. "Is he or isn't he Bobby Stone?"

"I doubt it, babe. But I'm willing to bet the mystery about the disappearance of Bobby is about to be solved."

Chapter Sixteen

Brynn thought Garrett had lost his mind. When she'd agreed to his suggestion they make s'mores, she'd figured they would roast the marshmallows in the wood-burning fireplace in his house, not outdoors in a fire pit in below-freezing nighttime temperatures in late-November Montana, when even the bears had probably gone into hibernation. Much to her delight, though, she noticed he'd turned on several outdoor portable propane heaters. His rationale: if she wanted to become a true Montanan, in order to survive the harsh winters, she had to thicken up her blood.

She lay under several alpaca throws between Garrett's outstretched legs on a cushioned recliner, savoring the warmth from his body and the heaters. "You continue to surprise me," Brynn said as she rested her head against his shoulder.

"This is only the beginning, babe. I have a lot more surprises planned for us."

"Us?"

"Yes, because there are so many things I want to experience with you."

She smiled. "Do want to tell me about them?"

"Not yet. What I don't want to do is repeat things you had with your exes."

"I doubt that." Brynn paused. "Unless you're into strip clubs."

"No, I'm not. Is that where they took you?"

A beat passed before Brynn revealed to Garrett that the man she'd been dating told her he'd wanted to surprise her for her birthday. The surprise had turned out to be a his-and-her strip club outing. He'd left her at the male stage while he'd gone to the one with women.

"Did you stay?" Garrett questioned.

"No. I waited outside. Needless to say, that was the beginning of the end of that relationship."

"He sounds like a real jerk."

Brynn snorted delicately. "Jerk doesn't begin to describe him. I must have been a magnet for jerks because a sixth sense told me not get involved with a rodeo performer again, but I'd ignored it and fell for one that wanted to keep our relationship secret. But in the end I was glad he'd insisted on that." She told him about the scandal involving his three baby mamas, two of whom were strippers. "Can you answer a question for me, Garrett?"

"What's that?"

"What's the allure of men sleeping with strippers without protection? Don't they know if they happen to get one pregnant, they're facing the possibly of a paternity suit?"

"That's something I can't answer for you, babe. I suppose it would be the same for women who are gold diggers. When they sleep with wealthy men or celebrities and have their babies, it's because they believe they can get big bucks in order to change their current lifestyle."

Brynn wanted to ask him about Faith. Had she been looking for those "big bucks"? Had she married him because he was an Abernathy, one of the wealthiest families not only in Bronco but also in Montana? She'd opened up to him about the men in her past and now she waited for Garrett to reveal some of the details of his failed marriage. She assumed that would be the next step, now that he'd gotten past his reluctance to date and held her hand, hugged her and attempted to steal a kiss in public.

Brynn wasn't willing to move forward in their relationship if they weren't able to let go of their pasts, which she had, or share their secrets. She'd already had one relationship with a secretive man and she did not want a repeat of that with Garrett.

But Garrett just lay quiet, wrapping his arms more tightly around her and kissing the top of her head. She decided he probably just needed more time. Spending this weekend together would make him feel more comfortable with her, she reasoned. She'd give Garrett another opportunity to open up to her about his failed marriage after she returned from Billings.

"Are you ready to go in?" he said in her ear.

"Yes." The snow that begun earlier that afternoon had stopped after an hour, leaving less than two inches on the ground, and it appeared like diamond dust under the glow of the full moon.

Brynn gathered the throws while Garrett shut off the fire pit and heaters. They walked in the house to find Max stretched out in front of the fireplace. Garrett removed the screen, stoked the dying embers and placed another log on the grate. He said Max would sleep there all night even after the fire went out completely.

"I'm going up to shower," she said to Garrett as he began turning off lights in the kitchen and dining area.

"I'll be up as soon as I lock up."

Brynn walked into the en suite bathroom and brushed her teeth before undressing and stepping into the free-standing shower. She undid the braid and stood under the spray of the oversized showerhead to shampoo her hair. She let out a shriek when the door opened and Garrett joined her. He was naked.

"What are you doing?"

Garrett flashed a sensual smile. "Saving water," he crooned as his hands cradled her breasts.

His head came down and he took her mouth in

a burning kiss that stole the breath from her lungs. One hand slipped lower over her belly as his fingers worked their magic between her thighs until she doubted whether her legs would support her.

Brynn felt as if she was on fire as she writhed against his wet body to get even closer. Throwing back her head, she screamed when an orgasm shook her, but Garrett didn't stop. He ignited her desire again and, within minutes, she was lost to the sensations his fingers evoked. It was only when she felt his erection against her belly that sanity returned.

"We have to stop, Garrett. We don't have any protection." She couldn't permit him to make love to her without a condom.

She must have gotten through to him because he raised his head and met her eyes. Recessed lights in the ceiling of the shower stall reflected off his gaze and seeing him look at her like that was a turn-on.

Then, without warning, he turned off the water and swept her up in his arms to carry her out of the shower and into the bedroom. He deposited her on the bed and, after slipping on a condom, he made love to her as if it was to be their last time.

Brynn screamed when a series of orgasms shook her from head to toe at the same time Garrett buried his face in the pillow under her head and groaned deep in his throat as they climaxed together. She lost track of the time as Garrett collapsed on top of her, their bodies spent, then he kissed her deeply before he got up to dispose of the condom. When he returned, she extended her arms to welcome him into the bed and symbolically into her life. Not only had she fallen in love Garrett Abernathy, but she also loved him with all of her heart.

The next two days felt as if they lived in an alternate universe. Garrett got up early as usual to do chores, while Brynn stay behind in the cabin, preparing brunch for his return, and he wasn't surprised when she'd admitted she like grilling outdoor in the winter. Using the grill saved them having to clean up the kitchen and provided more time for themselves. And for their lovemaking.

Garrett drove Brynn back to her apartment Sunday night, hoping his eyes communicated what he couldn't bring himself to say. He loved her. "Enjoy your stay in Billings," he said instead before kissing her.

Resting her hands on his chest over the corduroy jacket, she smiled up at him. "I'm only going to be away for a couple of days, so why are you making it sound as if it's going to be two weeks or even two months?"

"I'm going to miss you, Brynn."

"And I'm going to miss you, too."

Turning on his heel, he walked out of her apartment to where he'd parked his pickup.

During the drive to the Flying A, he replayed in his head everything he'd had with Brynn since being introduced to her the afternoon he'd gone to the Bronco Convention Center to meet with Chuck Carter about selling bison for the upcoming Mistletoe Rodeo. How much he enjoyed everything about Brynn Hawkins in and out of bed.

She was young, vibrant and beautiful. He'd also experienced twin emotions of pride and jealousy when men couldn't pull their gazes away from her at The Association fundraiser. And when he'd taken her home after the event, it should've been to make love to her, but he hadn't been given the opportunity when she'd practically closed the door in his face. Everything about the night was magical until they'd danced together during the heartbreaking love ballad "If I Didn't Love You."

A cold shudder ran up his back as the suspicion took hold. Did Brynn feel she would be better off without him if she didn't love him? But then he asked himself, did she love him? Garrett reminded himself that Brynn wasn't reticent about speaking her mind. If she truly did love him, wouldn't she have told him by now?

His thoughts and fears tumbled around inside his head so ferociously that a blinding pain stabbed his eyes. He slammed his hand on the steering wheel, ignoring the pain shooting up his arm. In fact, he welcomed it to keep from thinking about the woman who bewitched him and tied him in knots, and he knew he had to exorcise her not only from his head but also his heart.

Brynn returned to Bronco after spending two days in Billings. It had been the first time she'd been featured in a music video and realized it wasn't as glamourous behind the scenes as it looked on film.

She'd sent a text to her mother, sisters, and Garrett that she was back, and the taping was successful.

Remi and Corinne called to say they were coming over later that day because they wanted to hear all of the deets about the video shoot.

An hour later Garrett respond to her text.

Can you meet me at the barn? We need to talk.

I'm on my way.

Brynn thought about the shoot during the drive to the Flying A. Derrick Blackstone had recorded "Don't You Remember" with just an acoustic guitar and piano. His rendition was predicted to create as big a sensation for him as Whitney Houston when she'd covered Dolly Parton's "I Will Always Love You."

The four-minute video was divided into one-minute segments with her appearing differently in each one to coincide with the images of her in Derrick's memory. A stylist had washed and dried her curly hair with a diffuser attachment that gave her leonine look. She'd worn a white unbuttoned blouse with a hint of cleavage, body-hugging jeans and boots. When she'd stared directly into the camera lens, wearing dark dramatic eye makeup, the director had called it a wrap after one take.

The makeup artist had removed the makeup and she'd appeared almost virginal in a sundress and white tennis shoes, with her hair in two braids as she spun around while smiling at the videographer over her shoulder.

For the third segment, her hair had been brushed off her face into a ponytail and she'd reclined on the hood of pickup in revealing Daisy Duke cutoffs, a tank top and boots. It had taken four takes before she'd achieved the image the director had wanted. When she'd complained of fatigue, they'd halted the shoot so she should go back to her hotel and rest before returning later that night. They'd wanted to finish the shoot in one day.

When she'd returned to the studio, she'd discovered Derrick Blackstone on the set. Seeing him up close and in person made her aware why women were literally falling at his feet. He was the quintessential tall, dark, handsome, and had exuded a sexiness that was mesmerizing. He was to appear in the last segment in which he would be waiting for her to come to him. He'd kiss her, then, using special effects, she would disappear before his eyes.

She'd wanted to tell the director there was nowhere in the original script where she would be required to kiss the performer, but as her grandmother would say, she had to put on her big girl panties and roll with it.

Brynn had gone through another hair and makeup change when her curls were blown into full waves that framed her face, fell over her shoulders and down her back. She'd smiled when seeing the blood-red flowing satin gown with a sweetheart neckline. Dramatic black eyeshadow and vermilion lipstick made her feel sexy and naughty at the same time.

A fog machine created a dreamlike atmosphere as she'd walked barefoot toward where Derrick sat dressed entirely in black. She'd detected a shimmer of lust in his dark orbs, but she'd refused to fall under his sensual spell. She'd fallen for two men in the spotlight and, even if she wasn't in love with Garrett, she wasn't willing to go there again.

He'd risen to his feet with her approach and when they were mere inches apart he'd dipped his head to kiss her, and the director had called cut and that was a wrap. Brynn saw by Derrick's expression that he wasn't happy; she knew he'd wanted to actually kiss her.

The director complimented her, saying she was a natural and that he would love to work with her again on other videos. She'd told him the producer had her mother's number and he should talk to Josie.

The director then revealed that they were going to edit the tape overnight and have the sound engineer link it with the prerecorded lyrics because the record company wanted to release the video in two days.

When she'd told the director to contact her mother for upcoming gigs, Brynn hadn't been completely honest with the man. She was attempting to withdraw from the spotlight, accepting fewer events as one of the Hawkins Sisters. More than half her life had been recorded for posterity and now, at thirty, she was ready to turn the corner. She craved stability and privacy.

Brynn slowed down and maneuvered onto the road leading to the Flying A. It had only been two days since she'd seen Garrett, but for her it seemed longer, and she'd continued to ask herself how it had happened so quickly. How she'd come to need him when she'd never she needed man.

Want?

Yes.

Need?

Never.

And if anyone had asked her to describe herself, she would've said, "Independent, outspoken and supremely confident." Somehow, though, she couldn't imagine her life without Garrett now. And if he wanted to talk, so did she—about Faith.

She saw his pickup at the side of the barn, so she pulled up alongside it and shut off the engine. Her heart flip-flopped when she walked into the barn and saw him grooming a large stallion. He glanced up and she smiled. Brynn knew something was wrong when he didn't return her smile.

"What's up, Garrett?"

He gave the horse a carrot before setting the brush on a bench. "We need to talk."

Her eyes narrowed. "You said that in your text."

Garrett met her eyes. "I think we should think long and hard about what it would mean for the two of us to be together long-term."

"Why?" The query was flat, lacking emotion.

"Because not everyone will approve of our relationship because of our age difference."

"Now, we're back to that."

He took a step toward her then stopped. "What do you want with a man that's so much older than you?"

Brynn fisted her hands. "I don't have an issue with your age, and I don't give a damn what other people think about us."

"But I do." He paused. "And there's something else."

"What, Garrett?"

"Long distance relationships usually don't work. I'll be here while you'll spend more than half the year on the rodeo circuit coming and going by your leave."

Brynn counted slowly to five as she struggled not to lose her temper. "Are you making excuses because you're looking for a way out of our relationship?"

"Why would I want out?"

"I don't know, Garrett. Does it have something to do with Faith?" He recoiled as if she'd struck him when she'd mentioned the name, and Brynn decided to press her attack. "You were married to her, and apparently for a long time, yet you never talk about her."

"That's because that was in the past."

"Is it, Garrett? Really? Because if you're not willing to talk about her, then I don't believe she really is in the past. The only thing I'm going to say is thanks for the memories."

She turned on her heel and walked out of the barn before he could see the tears welling up in her eyes.

Brynn couldn't believe she was crying over a man when she never had before. When her prior relationships had ended, it had been good riddance to bad rubbish. But this time, with Garrett, it was different. Because she truly loved him.

She got into her vehicle and drove away from the Flying A. For the last time.

"You really know how to mess up a good thing."

Garrett turned to find Dean standing in the barn, arms crossed over his chest. He hadn't heard his brother when he'd entered. "What are you talking about?"

"Brynn, big brother. I heard what just happened. She's the best thing to come into your life, yet it's like you're afraid to be happy because you believe it will end like it did with you and Faith."

"Brynn isn't Faith."

"I'm glad you noticed, Garrett. So, what are you going to about it?"

"Nothing, Dean. And please mind your own business."

Dean threw up both hands. "Suit yourself, brother. But you know I love you and want to see you happy."

Garrett closed his eyes. He wanted to tell Dean he was happy, in fact gloriously happy with Brynn, but that's what frightened him. "Brynn does make me happy."

"Then what's the problem, Garrett?"

"The problem is it's not going to work–at least not long term." And he didn't want to tell Dean that he wasn't willing to repeat with Brynn what he'd had with Faith. "Brynn and I would be like two ships passing in the night and I need stability in my life. And right now Brynn Hawkins isn't that stability."

"What you need to do is think hard and long about what it would mean losing her–for good. But I know you told me to mind my own business, so I'm out," Dean said as he walked out of the barn.

Garrett picked up the brush and went back to grooming the stallion. He'd asked Brynn to meet him in the barn because he'd thought of it as neutral territory, far enough away from the cabin where he'd gone to bed and woken up with her beside him. He'd spent four glorious days with her, and Dean was right—he was afraid it would end much like his marriage. What had begun with hope and promise had slowly gone downhill, although he and Faith were living together they were living separate lives until he and Faith had barely tolerated each other's presence. That was something he didn't want for himself and Brynn. That she would eventually tire of spending so much time away from her older husband and ask for a divorce.

He loved Brynn, more than he could've imagined loving any woman, but knew ending their relationship now was for the best. It would save both of them heartache in the long run.

Remi and Corinne stared at each other then at Brynn. "Why does it seem as if you've lost your best friend when you just had a video shoot with one of the sexiest men on the planet?" Corinne asked.

Brynn had given her sisters the deets they'd asked for of the shoot, attempting to make it sound more exciting than she'd felt at that moment. She'd never lied to her sisters, and she didn't want to start now. "That's because I have lost him."

Corinne blinked. "Say what?"

"Garrett and I broke up."

"Why, Brynn?" Remi asked.

"Because he's stuck in the past, Remi. And I don't intend to compete with a woman or women from his past when I don't expect him to compete with the men from mine."

Reaching over, Corinne covered Brynn's hand with hers. "So, what are you going to do?"

"Move on."

"You just can't give up on him, Brynn. It's obvious his divorce has scarred him," Remi said.

"I can't be the only one fighting for our relationship. Garrett has to at least meet me halfway," she said, struggling not to cry in front of her sisters.

"And if he doesn't?" Corinne asked.

"I told you. I'm going to move on and that's that."

Corinne stood, Remi rising with her. "We're going to leave now. I'll call you in a couple of days to see if you're feeling better."

Brynn blinked back tears before they fell. "I'm good." And she was. She was good as long as she didn't dwell on what she'd had with Garrett. She'd fallen in love with him and, with time, the love would fade and she would be left with only the memories of what they'd shared together.

It was later that night when she lay in bed that she cried. She cried for what was and what she'd hoped to have with Garrett Abernathy – her happily ever after.

"Are you certain she said she was going to move on?" Dean asked Corinne.

"Yes," Remi confirmed.

Dean was shocked when Brynn's sisters had contacted him at Abernathy Meats and asked to meet with him and his brothers to stage an intervention between Brynn and Garrett. He'd set up a time for them to come when he knew Garrett would be at his cabin.

Weston leaned back in his chair in the conference room and rested a booted foot over the opposite knee. "Move on or move away from Bronco?"

Audrey glared at blue-eyed Weston Abernathy. "Does that really matter? My sisters claim she said it twice, and knowing Brynn, once she sets her mind to something, she rarely backs down. She has a month-to-month lease on her apartment at BH247 and if she doesn't renew it, then she will definitely leave Bronco."

"But what's going to happen to the Hawkins Sisters?" Crosby questioned.

"We're not going to break up because we live in different states or cities," Audrey said. "Let's keep the focus on Brynn and Garrett. What we have to do is get them together under some false pretenses before we go back on the circuit in a couple of weeks."

Tyler ran his fingers through his hair. "We better come up with something and quick."

Dean nodded. He recalled the conversation he'd had Garrett in the barn the day he broke up with Brynn. He was certain his brother was in love with her, but somehow could not forget what he'd had with his ex-wife. "I know it's not going to be easy, but between the seven of us, we should be able to think of something that should knock some sense into my muleheaded brother."

"Why don't you tell Garrett that Brynn is hooking up with another man?" Crosby suggested.

Tyler frowned at Crosby. "That won't work. Everybody knows she was hanging out at Garrett's cabin at night."

"I think Crosby is onto something," Remi said. "She just finished doing a video with Derrick Blackstone and we could say that Derrick wants her to go with him to the upcoming Houston Livestock Show and Rodeo that happens to be a three-week-long event where dozens of country stars are slated to play."

"Will the Hawkins Sisters be performing?" Tyler asked.

Audrey shook her head. "We're planning to skip it. That's why it's the perfect ruse to shake up Garrett. Brittany Dubois told me that Garrett glared at any man who stared at Brynn during The Association fundraiser. Even Daniel had mentioned it to his wife because he'd wanted to dance with Brynn but changed his mind when he saw Garrett's face."

"She did look hot in those photographs," Crosby said under his breath, garnering glares from everyone sitting around the table.

Dean sat straight. "So, you think her going out with Derrick Blackstone will do the trick?"

"We won't know if it will work if we don't put it out there," Remi said. "I follow Derrick Blackstone on social media and the music video is scheduled to drop in two days. And judging by what Brynn told us, it's very sexy."

Dean chuckled. "And probably sexy enough to make Garrett very, very jealous. Now, who's going to be responsible for telling my brother about Brynn hooking up with Derrick Blackstone?"

"I will," Crosby volunteered. "I'll tell him Remi called and told me."

"I suppose that settles it," Weston said as he exchanged fist bumps with everyone in the conference room.

Chapter Seventeen

Garrett paced the length of the porch like a big, caged cat. He knew he'd messed up—big-time—but he didn't know how to fix it. Not only did he miss Brynn, but he loved her. Loved her more than he'd ever loved anyone. He wanted their relationship to work—not only for himself but also for Brynn. But he'd been the one to destroy it.

Max ambled over and pushed his nose against his leg. Reaching down, he scratched the dog behind his ears. He hadn't taken more than a few steps when he heard the sound of an approaching vehicle. As it came closer, he recognized Crosby's pickup.

His brother had called and asked if he wanted to hang out at Doug's and that he would pick him up.

"Don't get out, Crosby. I need to put Max inside and make certain he has enough water."

Crosby turned off the Ford's engine and got out. "I need to show you something before we leave."

Garrett had no idea what that something was until he stood in the middle of the great room watching the music video on his brother's cell phone. The sound of Derrick Blackstone's mellifluous voice ceased to exist as he found himself hypnotized by the woman oozing sensuality in every frame. It was obvious she loved the camera as much as it loved her. The entire video had been shot in black-and-white except for the final scene where Brynn walked barefoot in the flowing, strapless, red gown that displayed more of her breasts than the one she'd worn to the fundraiser.

"What do you think, Garrett?"

He blinked as if coming out of a trance. "It's nice."

"Nice! She's freaking hot. I can't believe Brynn has been hiding those legs under her jeans."

"That's enough, Crosby!"

"Really, Garrett? It's a little late for you to act like the jealous boyfriend because the word is you broke up with her."

"Dean talks too much."

"Dean isn't the only one talking, big brother. Remi told me Brynn is moving on and that she's agreed to go on tour with Derrick Blackstone."

Garrett's expression became a mask of stone. He didn't want to believe Crosby. "Are you sure that's what she said?"

"Don't kill the messenger, Garrett."

"Why would Remi call you?"

"It's not what you think," Crosby countered. "I can be friends with a woman without hitting on her. And you shouldn't have a problem with Brynn dating Blackstone because she doesn't have a ring on her finger. A woman's left hand is like a traffic light. If it's bare, then the light is green and that means you can go for her. A promise or engagement ring is a blinking yellow caution light. And a wedding band is red and that means stop. The last time I saw Brynn's left hand, it was a green light."

Garrett knew his brother was right. Brynn was a single woman, and she could date whomever she pleased—anyone but Derrick Blackstone. The man had been linked to so many women that Garrett knew Brynn would become just another notch on his belt.

"Do you mind if I don't go with you to Doug's tonight?" he asked Crosby.

"Come on, bro. I was really looking forward to hanging out with you tonight."

"I'm sorry, Crosby, but I have to take care of some unfinished business."

"Does that business have anything to do with a curly haired, long-legged woman?"

Garrett forced a smile he didn't quite feel, praying he wasn't too late to make things right between him and Brynn. "Yes, it does."

"In that case, I don't mind the brush-off." Crosby gave his shoulder a soft punch. "Go get your woman, and you better talk a good game or you're going to lose her to Derrick Blackstone."

"That's not happening."

Crosby nodded. "If you need any more advice from the love doctor, you know how to reach me."

"Get the hell outta here so I can go and salvage what's left of my love life."

"You love Brynn?"

"Go home, Crosby."

"Later, bro."

Brynn sat on the sofa, her legs tucked under her body as she watched the local news. Derrick's video had been released earlier that morning and she'd viewed it three time before switching the channel.

Her cell phone rang and she glanced at the screen. It was a number she didn't recognize, but decided to answer it. "Hello?"

"We need to talk."

"Garrett? Where are you calling me from?"

"I'm downstairs in your parking lot. I'm calling from the Abernathy Meats' private line. As I said, we need to talk."

"No, Garrett. *You* need to talk and until you're ready to do that, please don't contact me again."

"Why? Because you're hooking up with Derrick Blackstone?"

"Who told you that?"

"Let me in and I'll tell you." He hesitated a second then, "I'll tell you everything—and that includes what happened between me and Faith."

Brynn's heart was beating so fast that she suddenly felt light-headed. She'd been waiting and praying since their last encounter that Garrett would open up about his ex-wife, because they couldn't talk about a future together if they couldn't get beyond the past.

"Give me five minutes to put some clothes on, then you can come up."

"You don't have to put anything on, Brynn. Remember I've seen you naked before."

"Five minutes, Garrett."

She ended the call, raced to the bedroom to take off a pair of pajamas and slip into a sweatshirt and jeans, and ran a wide-toothed comb through her tangled curls at the same time the doorbell rang. She opened the door and stood off to the side to let Garrett enter.

Garrett reached for Brynn's left hand and kissed the back of it. In his mind. he replayed Crosby's statement about a woman's hand. Brynn's was bare, which meant a green light. She could go and be with any man she chose.

The only man Garrett wanted her with was him.

"Will you come home with me?"

"Why, Garrett? Why can't we talk here?"

He led her into the living room, easing her down to sit with him on the love seat. "After I tell you everything about my life with Faith, I'd like you to come home with me. I'm asking because I've missed going to bed and waking up with you. And because I love you more than I've ever loved anyone, and I'm willing to do whatever I have to do to make our relationship work."

Brynn blinked. "You love me?"

"I know there are times when I find it hard to say

it, but what I try to do is show you how much I love you and want you in my life. That is, if you want me."

"How can you be so obtuse, Garrett Abernathy? I never would've asked you to kiss me or to make love to me if I didn't love you."

"But what about you going on tour with Derrick Blackstone?"

"What are you talking about?"

Garrett took off his Stetson and tunneled his fingers through his hair. He blew out a shaky breath. At that point, even he didn't know what he was talking about anymore. All he knew was that he had to get things off his chest. Things like his past.

Before he answered her question, he took Brynn back over two decades, telling her everything from dating Faith in high school to marrying her after college to living in New York City. He told her about the breakup of his marriage and why he'd had to return to Bronco and resume his life as a rancher. Recounting everything left him feeling raw and exposed, but Brynn had a right to know what had made him the man he was. Then, finally, he told her what Crosby had told him about her and Derrick Blackstone.

Brynn laughed. "There's no way I would go anywhere with Derrick Blackstone. I told you I'd had enough of rodeo cowboys and celebrity types. I did that video because my mother wanted another venue to promote her daughters. I told her it was the first and last time for me. I also told her I wouldn't commit to performing in as many rodeos as in the past because I want to concentrate on growing my business."

"Does this mean you're not leaving Bronco?"

"No, Garrett, I'm not leaving. Why would I?"

He smiled. "Just asking, because Crosby was told you said you were moving on."

"Wait a minute. Crosby told you some nonsense about me hooking up with Derrick, then that I was moving on? I meant I was moving on with my life and not leaving Bronco. Something tells me my sisters and your brothers cooked up this scheme to get us back together."

Garrett couldn't believe he'd been duped. "Do you think we should confront them?"

"No, because it worked, didn't it?"

"Yes. I owe them my thanks. They saved me from making the biggest mistake of my life if I'd lost you."

"Well, you didn't lose me, Garrett, because I'm not one to cut and run. I was willing to wait for you to come to your senses to realize what you were losing because of your stiff-necked pride. I'm not your ex-wife and not in any way do I want to be compared to her."

"That will never happen," he said as he pressed his lips against hers.

Brynn pushed against his chest. "You're going to have to let me go so I can pack some clothes if I'm going home with you."

Garrett waited for Brynn to go into her bedroom before he pumped the air with both fists. If it hadn't been for the meddling of his brothers and Brynn's sisters, he would have lost the woman who had turned his life upside down—and for the best. He felt a gentle peace because Brynn had admitted she loved him as much as he loved her, and now it was time for them to plan for a future together.

It was December first, the night of the tree lighting ceremony, and it was as if all of Bronco had turned out to celebrate. It was to become Brynn's first Christmas in Bronco and the excitement was palpable as she strolled the crowded sidewalks with Garrett on their way to Sadie's Holiday House where he claimed he wanted to get her a special present. He knew she'd been eyeing a teddy bear with a Santa hat, but she'd forgotten to pick it up because she'd been too busy concentrating on buying gifts for her family. They walked in and Sadie greeted them, smiling.

"What happened with that man the other day?" Garrett asked Sadie.

She sighed and shook her head. "That's a long story, Garrett. Too long to talk about now. If you come with me, I'll show you what you said you're looking for."

Brynn smiled at Garrett. "I'll be here when you get back. I'm going to do a little more shopping because I'd like to pick up something for Lola and Maeve." She'd planned to give both girls machine-stitched quilted blankets with squares of alphabet letters and corresponding animals, because there wasn't enough time to hand-stitch them. Her future plans included making quilts for Callie, Susanna and Everlee as wedding gifts. It'd only been two days since she and Garrett had reconciled, and it was as if there hadn't been a pause in their relationship.

She wandered into the room filled with Kwanzaa items and she picked up a kinara along with the different colored candles to celebrate the cultural holiday. If she and Garrett were going to be together, then it was time for him to become familiar with some African American customs.

A salesclerk had processed her purchases, wrapped everything in tissue paper, and just put them into a shopping bag when Garrett joined her. "Did you find what you wanted?" she asked him.

"Yes. How about you? Are you finished shopping?"

"Yes. I bought the items we need to celebrate Kwanzaa."

"Good."

"You know about Kwanzaa?"

"Of course."

"All right, cowboy. I'll look for you to tell me about the seven principles of Kwanzaa because I've forgotten a few."

Reaching for her hand, Garrett led her out of the shop and down a block to where the crowd had thinned out. He stopped under a streetlight and pulled a small box from the pocket of his jacket. Brynn gasped when he opened it and numbly stared at cushion-cut emerald surrounded by a halo of diamonds.

"When Sadie told me she had a small collection of estate pieces, I asked her to show me what she had. And when I saw this ring, I knew I wanted to give it to you. It's a promise ring to cherish you always and to make you my wife when the time is right."

Brynn couldn't stop her left hand from shaking when Garrett slipped the ring on her finger. "There is no time like the present, Garrett. I love you so much, and I would be thrilled to marry you and have your babies, if that's what you want."

"It's exactly what I want. I want as many babies as you're willing to give me, and a few more when we continue the Hawkins' tradition of adopting. I'll have a contractor build you a workshop on the property, where you can make your crafts and sell them in a shop in the business district. And if you want horses, then I'll ask Daniel Dubois if he's willing to sell some to me."

"When did you figure all of this out?"

"The night I was able to let go of my past to plan a future for us."

Brynn leaned into Garrett and kissed him. "I like your plans."

He increased the pressure on her mouth when he deepened the kiss. "I was hoping you would say that."

Brynn spread out her fingers, smiling as the streetlight reflected off the diamonds. She couldn't believe everything she'd ever wanted was falling into place, and for that she was thankful for her cowboy.

* * * * *

#2947 THE MAVERICK'S CHRISTMAS SECRET
Montana Mavericks: Brothers & Broncos • by Brenda Harlen
Ranch hand Sullivan Grainger came to Bronco to learn the truth about his twin's disappearance. All he's found so far is more questions—and an unexpected friendship with his late brother's sister-in-law, Sadie Chamberlin. The sweet and earnest shopkeeper offers Sullivan a glimpse of how full his life could be, if only he could release the past and embrace Sadie's Christmas spirit!

#2948 STARLIGHT AND THE CHRISTMAS DARE
Welcome to Starlight • by Michelle Major
Madison Maurer is trying to be content with her new life working in a small town bar but is still surprised when her boss-mandated community work leads to some unexpected friendships, including a teenage delinquent. The girl's older brother is another kind of surprise—and they're all in need of some second chances this Christmas!

#2949 THEIR TEXAS CHRISTMAS MATCH
Lockharts Lost & Found • by Cathy Gillen Thacker
A sudden inheritance stipulates commitment-phobes Skye McPherson and Travis Lockhart must marry and live together for a hundred and twenty days. A quick, temporary marriage is clearly the easiest solution. Until Skye discovers she's pregnant with her new husband's baby and Travis starts falling for his short-term wife. With a million reasons to leave, will love win out this Christmas?

#2950 LIGHTS, CAMERA...WEDDING?
Sutter Creek, Montana • by Laurel Greer
Fledgling florist Bea Halloran has banked her business and love life on her upcoming reality TV Christmas wedding. When her fiancé walks out, Bea's best friend, Brody Emerson, steps in as the fake groom, saving her business...and making her feel passion she barely recognizes. And Brody's smoldering glances and knee-weakening kisses might just put their platonic vows to the test...

#2951 EXPECTING HIS HOLIDAY SURPRISE
Gallant Lake Stories • by Jo McNally
Jade is focused on her new bakery and soon, raising her new baby. When Jade's one-night stand, Trent Mitchell, unexpectedly shows up, it's obvious that their chemistry is real. Until Jade's fierce independence clashes with Trent's doubts about fatherhood. Is their magic under the mistletoe strong enough to make them a forever family?

#2952 COUNTERFEIT COURTSHIP
Heart & Soul • by Synithia Williams
When a kiss at a reality TV wedding is caught on camera, there's only one way to save *his* reputation and *her* career. Now paranormal promoter Tyrone Livingston and makeup artist Kiera Fox are officially dating. But can a relationship with an agreed-upon end date turn into a real and lasting love?

YOU CAN FIND MORE INFORMATION ON UPCOMING HARLEQUIN TITLES, FREE EXCERPTS AND MORE AT HARLEQUIN.COM.

SPECIAL EXCERPT FROM

◆ HARLEQUIN
SPECIAL EDITION

*Madison Mauer is trying to be content with her new
life working in a small-town bar but is still surprised
when her boss-mandated community work leads to
some unexpected friendships, including a teenage
delinquent. The girl's older brother is another kind
of surprise—and they're all in need of some second
chances this Christmas!*

*Read on for a sneak peek at
Starlight and the Christmas Dare,
the next book in the Welcome to Starlight miniseries
by* USA TODAY *bestselling author Michelle Major!*

"I'm going to call my friend who's a nurse in the morning.
She's not working in that capacity now, but she grew up
in this town. She'll help get you with a good physical
therapist."

The warmth she'd seen in his eyes disappeared, and
she told herself it shouldn't matter. It was better they
remember who they were to each other—people who had
a troubled girl in common but nothing more.

She couldn't allow it to be anything more.

"You need a Christmas tree," he said as she started to
back away.

"I didn't see any decorations in your house."

HSEEXP1022

He nodded. "Yeah, but Stella made me promise I would at least get a tree."

"I'll consider a tree," Madison told him. It felt like a small concession. "Although I'm not much for Christmas spirit."

"That makes two of us."

Once again, she wasn't sure how to feel about having something in common with Chase.

He cleared his throat. "I have more work to do—meetings and deadlines to reschedule. I can make it back to the bedroom."

"I'll see you tomorrow."

"I'll be here." He laughed without humor. "It's not like I can get anywhere else."

"Good night, Chase."

"Good night, Madison," he answered.

The words felt close to a caress, and she hurried to her bedroom before her knees started to melt.

Don't miss
Starlight and the Christmas Dare *by Michelle Major,*
available December 2022 wherever
Harlequin Special Edition books and ebooks are sold.

Harlequin.com

HARLEQUIN
PLUS

Announcing a **BRAND-NEW** multimedia subscription service for romance fans like you!

Read, Watch and Play.

Experience the easiest way to get the romance content you crave.

Start your **FREE 7 DAY TRIAL** at
<u>www.harlequinplus.com/freetrial</u>.